U0127326

國際安徒生插畫大獎

周年展

Hans Christian
Andersen Awards
50 th Anniversary Exhibition

目次
CONTENTS

《所有微小的關心！》羅傑梅洛
2014安徒生插畫大獎得主

"Todo Cuidado é Pouco!" Roger Mello
2014 Hans Christian Andersen Award Winner

序 / PREFACE

素有兒童文學諾貝爾獎之稱的國際安徒生大獎，如同諾貝爾獎一樣是終生成就獎項，每兩年由聯合國教科文組織下的IBBY(International Board on Books for young People)頒發給對於兒童文學有所貢獻的童書作家及插畫家。

1956年創辦後，一開始只設有作家獎項，但隨著圖畫書創作成為視覺思考的重新探索，吸引了越來越多藝術學院學生的投入，繪本也隨之蓬勃發展，自1966年起新增插畫家獎項，「國際安徒生插畫大獎」（Hans Christian Andersen Awards for illustration）應勢而生。

難得的是，這些獲獎的大師們，有些擁有自己的美術館，有些早已多次舉辦個人大型展覽，卻從未在「國際安徒生插畫大獎」的光環下共同舉辦展覽。去年我們策劃了「波隆納世界插畫大展」，將睽違台灣15年的插畫界奧斯卡獎帶回台灣的觀眾面前，吸引了12萬人參觀。台灣觀眾對於插畫的熱情支持，超出我們的預期，更讓遠在義大利波隆納的兒童書展主辦單位深受感動，國際插畫界開始對「台灣」充滿了肯定。當我們向IBBY主席Wally de Doncker提出舉辦「國際安徒生插畫大獎」作為50週年慶祝，儘管台灣並非聯合國教科文組織的會員國，但他對於近年來兒童文學與插畫推廣在台灣的盛況早有所聞，因此大力支持本展，也讓台北順利成為「國際安徒生插畫大獎」的國際巡展第一站。

有了「國際安徒生插畫大獎」官方主辦單位的支持，要一一說服25位插畫大師參展並非易事，半世紀的大獎歷史代表著早期得獎者也步入歷史。幸運的是，我們邀請到知名的國際插畫出版人Michael Neugebauer擔任展覽顧問，透過他長年在兒童繪本界的耕耘與豐厚人脈關係，我們逐一與得獎者或是其繼承人、美術館與私人藏家聯繫上，將這個看似不可能的任務圓滿達成。

「國際安徒生大獎」的創設宗旨在於兒童文學的鼓勵，藉由優美的文字與生動的圖像，建立小小讀者們的正面價值觀。繪本的影響力不僅止於此，透過圖畫的共通語言，不僅是兒童，大人也從中探索人生的意義。

「國際安徒生插畫大獎50週年展」將引領我們，回顧這半世紀中國際上偉大的插畫大師創作，各具特色的筆觸與構圖，充滿個人想像的詮釋。在這裡，我們邀請每位觀眾全心感受美好圖像帶來的感染力與影響力。

王玉齡
蔚龍藝術有限公司 總經理

The Hans Christian Andersen Award has been known as the Nobel Prize of children's literature. It is a biennial award and also a lifetime achievement as the Nobel Prize announced by the International Board on Books for young People, IBBY, the foundation under the UNESCO. The award is specialized for authors and illustrators who have built great contributions in children's literature.

After the foundation in 1956, the writing award was the only announced one. Because the creations of pictures books have become a new exploration of visual thinking. More and more students from art schools have been involving in creating picture books, and the picture books has flourished along with it. The illustration award was inaugurated since 1966. The Hans Christian Andersen Awards for illustration has been known as a reputation for the occasion.

The most precious one is that those winners of the Hans Christian Andersen Awards for illustration have not held an exhibition together before, even some of them having their own museums, some of them having been the hosts of their personal exhibitions. We planned the Bologna Illustrators Exhibition for bringing the award which has been known as the Oscars of illustration back to Taiwan after a 15-year- long vacuum. More than 120,000 visitors has been attracted by the occasion. The enthusiastic reflection towards illustrations of Taiwanese people is against to all expectations. The organizer of the 2015 Bologna Children's Book Fair based in Bologna has also been moved by the reflection of Taiwanese people. The experts of illustration started to praise on Taiwanese audiences. We applied the International Exhibit of Hans Christian Andersen Awards for illustration for the 50 anniversary, the President of IBBY, Wally de Doncker who has heard about the grand occasion of the promotion in children's literature and illustration even though Taiwan doesn't have a membership in UNESCO. He strongly supports this plan and makes Taipei become the first station of the traveling exhibition of the Hans Christian Andersen Awards for illustration.

Even though we gained the mighty support by the official organizer, it was not an easy job about convincing 25 masters of illustration to join the exhibit. And also, the 50-year-long history means that some of the early winners has departed from this world. Fortunately, we have invited the famous publisher in the world, Michael Neugebauer as our exhibition consultant. We successful contacted the winners(or the winners' offspring), museums and collectors by his good relationship in children's picture books and complete the mission looks impossible.

The purpose of the Hans Christian Andersen Award is encouraging children's literature. Children's literature will help children build the positive principles by sophisticated words and vigorous pictures. The above is not the only effect by picture books. Not only children, but adults could also explore the meaning of life by graphics, the common language in the world.

The 50 anniversary Exnibition of the Hans Christian Andersen Awards for illustration will guide us. Reviewing the masterpieces of illustration in the past 50 years, we will feel the characteristic brushwork and layouts, the self-imaging interpretation. We invite every audience to here to feel the appealing and effectiveness of elegant illustrations.

Yuling Wang
General Manager, Blue Dragon Art Company

「為什麼諾貝爾文學獎只頒給成人？」國際兒童讀物聯盟(IBBY)創辦人Jella Lepman於其著作《童書之橋》(A Bridge of Children's Books)中提出了這個疑問。50年代初期，對於兒童文學應設有類似獎項的討論越趨熱烈，催生了國際安徒生大獎(Hans Christian Andersen Awards)。

60年來，國際安徒生大獎一直是兒童讀物作家和插畫家的最高榮譽，幕後推手是丹麥女王瑪格麗特二世，目前主要贊助單位為韓國南怡島公司，得獎候選人則由IBBY國家組(National Sections)負責提名。2016年國際安徒生大獎的頒發，吸引全球媒體目光，顯示本獎的魅力和公信力仍持續增長。

國際安徒生大獎可說是兒童文學界唯一真正全球性的獎項，由來自世界各地兒童文學專家所組成的國際評審團挑選出得獎者。評審團每次召開會議時都會討論遴選標準：文字、插畫的美學、文學質感，作家或插畫家是否能從孩子的角度看待事物，能否讓孩子延伸好奇心和想像力等，都是評選考量。

國際安徒生大獎的歷史漫長且有趣。1958年阿思緹林格倫(Astrid Lindgren)在義大利佛羅倫斯的IBBY大會中獲頒本獎，由於本獎受到高度重視，義大利總統甚至為此搭直升機飛到會場頒獎給她。許多知名童書創作者都是國際安徒生大獎得主：埃利希克斯特納(Erich Kästner)、石田道雄(Michio Mado)、莉絲白茨威格(Lisbeth Zwerger)、凱薩琳帕特森(Katherine Paterson)、湯米溫格爾(Tomi Ungerer)、英諾桑提(Roberto Innocenti)、彼德席斯(Peter Sis)，今年文學獎及插畫獎得主分別是曹文軒(Cao Wenxuan)和貝爾納(Rotraut Susanne Berner)。

國際安徒生大獎一開始只頒給作家；但1966年，也就是本獎設立十年後，國際安徒生大獎新增了插畫家的專屬獎項。究竟為什麼插畫在60年代開始受到重視呢？是否和獨立青年運動崛起有關？還是和兒童解放有關？或是當時為繪本插畫奠定基礎的新銳藝術家們才是主因？最佳例子便是1963年，莫里斯桑達克(Maurice Sendak)在《野獸國》(Where The Wild Things Are)裡描繪了一個充滿虛構兇猛怪獸的超現實世界。60年代中期開始出現以插畫為主、文字為輔的新型態繪本，艾瑞卡爾(Eric Carle)於1967年出版的《棕色的熊、棕色的熊，你在看什麼？》(Brown Bear, Brown Bear, What Do You See?)，由色紙拼貼而成、色彩明亮、創作形式大膽的繪本首次問世。

如今繪本風行全球。諷刺的是，平淡無趣是繪本最大的危險，而正因為繪本市場的全球化發展，大型國際出版商為了顧及市場，反倒越來越常出版無趣且尺寸單一的兒童讀物和青少年讀物。兒童文學正面臨文化認同消失的危機。

因此，透過「國際安徒生插畫大展」提升歷屆得獎作品的能見度，我們必須團結起來，對抗兒童和青少年文學日益商業化的趨勢，不應該把這群年輕讀者當作商品。我們要給孩子優質文學和插畫作品，他們值得最好的。

Wally De Doncker
國際兒童讀物聯盟主席

"Why should only adult books be considered for the Nobel Prize?" asked Jella Lepman, the founder of IBBY in her book "A Bridge of Children's Books". At the start of the fifties it was high time for there to be a similar prize given for literature for children, so ran the thinking that brought about the Hans Christian Andersen Awards.

For sixty years the Hans Christian Andersen Award has been the highest international recognition given to an author and an illustrator of children's books. The Patron of the Andersen Awards is Her Majesty Queen Margrethe II of Denmark and Nami Island Inc., from the Korean Republic is the current sponsor of the Awards. The candidates for the Awards are nominated exclusively by the National Sections of IBBY. In 2016, the Hans Christian Andersen Awards captured remarkable attention of the world's press showing how its appeal and integrity is still growing.

The Andersen Awards can be described as the only true world awards for children's literature: the winners are selected by a distinguished international jury of children's literature specialists from the different regions of the world. The jury discusses the selection criteria every time it convenes, and always include the aesthetic and literary qualities of writing and illustrating as well as the ability to see things from the child's point of view and the ability to stretch a child's curiosity and imagination.

The history of the Hans Christian Andersen Awards is long and interesting. Astrid Lindgren received her Award at the IBBY Congress in 1958 in Florence, Italy. The Award was seen to be so important that the President of Italy flew by helicopter to present her medal at the ceremony. Many prestigious creators of children's books are Andersen laureates: Erich Kästner, Michio Mado, Lisbeth Zwerger, Katherine Paterson, Tomi Ungerer, Roberto Innocenti, Peter Sis and this year's recipients Cao Wenxuan and Rotraut Susanne Berner.

The Hans Christian Andersen Awards began with a single award given to an author, but ten years later in 1966 an Andersen Award was also established for illustrators. Why exactly was there a shift in appreciation for illustrators during the sixties? Did it have anything to do with the ascent of an independent youth movement? The liberation of the child? Or was it the innovative artists who laid down the foundations for illustrated books for children. Such as, Maurice Sendak in 1963 with his book Where The Wild Things Are, depicting a surreal and menacing world of make-believe creatures. In the mid-1960s a new kind of picture book emerged in which the illustrations dominated the text. Eric Carle's bright, bold collages made from painted tissue paper debuted in 1967 with Brown Bear, Brown Bear, What Do You See?

The picture book now flourishes around the globe. It is ironic that the greatest danger to picture books is blandness. Big international publishers are tending to produce insipid one-size-fits-all books for children and young people that cater for the development of the ever-globalizing market. Cultural identity is in danger of vanishing from children's literature.

Here lies the necessity for the Hans Christian Andersen Awards that are highlighted by this prestigious exhibition. We must present a front against the increasing commercialization of children's and youth literature. We must refuse to consider young readers as commercial products. We want to cherish them by giving them quality literature and illustrations because only the best is good enough for children.

Wally De Doncker
President of IBBY

卡瑞吉特
ALOIS CARIGIET

瑞士   SWITZERLAND

1966

卡瑞吉特(1902-1985)生於瑞士格勞賓登州的小村特倫(Trun)，一個食指浩繁的農家，11個孩子中排行第七。由於務農謀生困難，卡瑞吉特的父親在格勞賓登州的首府庫爾(Chur)找到工作，舉家遷移到大城;那次搬家帶給9歲的卡瑞吉特極大衝擊，由羅曼語區搬到德語區，且是從「山上男孩的天堂」到「城市窄巷中的陰暗公寓」，天壤之別，簡直像是一場移民。

在庫爾接受裝飾藝術與設計的訓練之後，卡瑞吉特搬到蘇黎世，廣告、海報、雜誌封面都屢屢獲獎。1939年，卡瑞吉特毅然放棄蘇黎世經營得有聲有色的事業，決定回歸他所懷念的大自然，搬到格勞賓登州的山區農舍，成為自由工作者，專心致力於繪畫和素描創作。

卡瑞吉特的繪本之路始於1940年代。以羅曼語創作的瑞士作家賽琳娜・柯恩斯(Selina-Chonz)邀請卡瑞吉特為她所寫的故事合作繪本，卡瑞吉特幾經猶豫，終於完成他的成名之作，《提著小鈴鐺的烏利》(Schellen-Ursli)於1945年出版，1950年出版英文版《A Bell for Ursli》，成為全球長銷50萬本的經典名著。

柯恩斯住在優美古老的小鎮瓜爾達(Guarda)，她以當地著名的春季節慶–驅走寒冬的趕雪節「牛鈴遊行」(Chalandamarz)作為故事舞台，創造出充滿勇氣的勵志故事。小男孩烏利勇闖高山教堂，一心想要獲得最大的牛鈴，走在遊行隊伍最前端，經歷大自然的壯闊美景、離家出走的小探險、山間星空下的孤寂、父母的焦慮、回到溫暖、安全的家...卡瑞吉特以圖畫記錄逐漸消失的傳統生活，曾經存在於現實中的世界，已漸漸變成童話中的遙遠國度。

卡瑞吉特擅用自然流暢的線條、鮮艷而渾厚的色彩，勾勒濃濃的阿爾卑斯風情，他與柯恩斯延續烏利的冒險之旅，合作繪本《莉娜與野鳥》(Florina-and the Wild Bird)、《大雪》(Snowstorm)等系列作品，被稱為卡瑞吉特的瑞士三部曲。1960年代，卡瑞吉特轉為自寫自畫，講述童年記憶的故事，以三隻小羊為主角的《蓬蓬、小小與矮矮》(Zottel, Zick und Zwerg)充滿溫馨的鄉村人情味，為卡瑞吉特贏得1966年瑞士童書獎(Swiss Youth Book Prize)，同年，國際安徒生大獎將獎勵繪本插畫終生成就的第一項桂冠，授予卡瑞吉特。

熱愛家鄉風土，卡瑞吉特生命中的最後二十餘年都定居特倫，在寧謐山村以繪畫守護著歐洲最小的語區以及羅曼文化傳統。卡瑞吉特曾說他的創作是抽象時代中的「敍事性藝術」(narrative-art)，而他所創造的小男孩烏利，則像阿爾卑斯山的少女海蒂一樣，成為無數孩子的共同回憶。

Alois Carigiet (1902-1985) was born in Truns in Canton Grisons and grew up in a peasant family of ten children. He finished his training as a painter and decorator in Chur, the canton's capital, and later moved to Zurich. After seventeen years of successful work in advertising, stage design and applied graphics, he moved back to his mountains and began to dedicate himself solely to freelance painting and drawing. From this time on, both became the media for the expression of his feelings and thoughts. The spontaneity of his message, his technical skill and use of colour quickly earned him a good reputation among the painters of his generation.

Carigiet was already established among the leading artists in Switzerland when the poet and teacher Selina Chonz asked him in 1945 to illustrate a story in verse which she had written for her pupils. Selina Chonz wrote in Romansh and German and lived in one of Switzerland's prettiest villages, Guarda in the Engadine. In Guarda, as in many other villages in the canton, it was customary to ring in the spring with cow bells. The children walked through the streets ringing their bells, and each child wanted to have the biggest and loudest bell. The first picture book by Carigiet, *Schellen-Ursli(A Ball for Ursli)* in 1945, was based on this motif. The wild beauty of nature, the adventure of a little runaway, the loneliness of a starry night in the mountains, the anxiety of his parents, his return to the wonderful secu-rity of a warm home – all these are dealt with here with matchless freshness. With Carigiet's work, a vanishing world was captured in both words and pictures. What was reality a few years ago is gradually retreating to the far-away land of fairy tale.

Florina and the Wild Bird and *The Snowstorm*, with verses by the same author, varied the theme with other adventures and added other characters to that of Ursli. These three volumes later became known as his Swiss trilogy.

With *Anton the Goatherd* in 1965, Carigiet began a new series of picture books, including three volumes derived from his own childhood memories, with his own texts. In addition to picture books Carigiet also illustrated school readers for the canton of Zurich and fairy tales of the Grisons, ad well as Jck London's *Call of the Wild* and other texts.

Carigiet's picture books, specially *A Bell for Ursli*, have been published worldwide. Love for the little boy with the big bell unites children, as did Heidi and the other child characters of the Swiss mountain world many years ago. It is an extraordinary thought that one of the most important picture books of the twentieth century derives its strength and power, its language and its teality from a part of a region that represents one of the smallest language areas of Europe.

A Bell for Ursli
提著小鈴鐺的烏利

傑利唐卡
JIŘÍ TRNKA

捷克共和國　CZECH REPUBLIC

1968

傑利唐卡(1912-1969)逝於布拉格的前一年，獲頒國際安徒生大獎桂冠，表彰他對童書繪本的貢獻。然而，在他57年的精采一生，比童書繪本更勝一籌的成就是偶戲，更在捷克的偶動畫界具有開創、領導的崇高地位。

1912年生於波西米亞西部小鎮比爾森(Pilsen)，傑利唐卡自幼酷愛操作人偶，正好他的中學老師是日後成為捷克偶戲泰斗的人偶師舒庫巴(Josef Skupa)，帶引傑利唐卡深入瞭解偶戲，並鼓勵他進入布拉格應用藝術學院。

唐卡自1937年投入繪本創作，同時致力於發展偶戲劇場，1945年正式從事動畫創作，進而於1946年與捷克早期的幾位動畫大師共同組成偶動畫工作室Bratriv Triku(1969年更名為傑利唐卡工作室以茲紀念)，成為深耕捷克偶動畫創作的開山巨擘。

法國劇作家尚考克多(Jean Cocteau)曾讚譽傑利唐卡是「能夠形塑夢想和童年的魔術師」。不論偶劇、動畫、繪本，唐卡經常取材莎士比亞、歌德、格林兄弟、拉封丹、安徒生、威廉豪夫等大師之作，以及不少捷克知名作家作品，卻都能跳脫窠臼，展現「傑利唐卡風」的圖像魅力。

他的畫作有股獨特的抒情詩意，伴隨著激情與戲劇張力，讓人清楚感受到，他的根基來自捷克傳統的人文底蘊。幾乎沒有任何一個捷克兒童，成長過程中沒接觸過唐卡的作品，捷克繪本大師莉絲白茨威格更因受到傑利唐卡作品的感召，才走上繪本創作之路。

唐卡企圖讓插畫內化為作品的一部份，使圖畫變成包含文字的有機體，以激發孩子的想像力。「直截了當的童書常給我一種很淺薄的感覺，我從未用這種方式創作。我為每一本童書所畫的插畫，都是我在創作時的終極目標，我為它們盡我所能付出一切。」

唐卡畢生創作130餘件繪本作品，經典再詮釋之外，也曾自寫自畫，1962年作品《穿越魔法之門》(The Enchanted Gate)就是膾炙人口的代表作。繪本創作往往也激發傑利‧唐卡創作動畫的靈感，改編自哈薩克經典故事的《好兵帥克》(The Good Soldier Schweik)就是唐卡動畫擄獲捷克觀眾的人氣之作。

終戰之後的捷克動盪不安，可說是創作者的黑暗國度。傑利唐卡1965年創作的動畫《魔手》(Ruka)，描述政治對藝術創作的高度控制與打壓，此後再無作品;1968年，唐卡獲頒國際安徒生大獎，也正是捷克紅軍武力鎮壓，史稱「布拉格之春」的一年;1969年，傑利唐卡去世，《魔手》則被禁長達20年。

Jiří Trnka was born in Pilsen in 1912 and died in Prague in 1969. From an early age he was preoccupied with puppets, an interest that was stimulated further when he went to school, since his drawing teacher was one of Czecho-Slovakia's leading puppeteers. Thanks to this teacher he was able to study at the Prague School of Applied Art.

Trnka became know as 'The Puppet Wizard'. Dolls appear everywhere in his work. He undertook original and pioneering work with puppet plays, magic lantern shows, set designs and costumes, film cartoons and anima-tions – being Disney's only genuine European rival in the forties. ''Jiří Trnka is a magician who is able to give form to the dreams of childhood'' , as Jean Cocteau put it. Trnka himself said: ''Every work of creative art is an artistic stylisation of reality...Every artist has his particular way if seeing things, his views and method of stylization. If my figures resemble puppets, that's a feature of the style that is characteristic of my work.''

Both in the puppet theatre, in animated and cartoon films, and as a book illustrator, he worked on the great classics: Shakespeare, Goethe, Grimm, La Fontaine, Andersen, Hauff, as well as on a series of well-known Czech classics and popular writers such as Hasek, Hrubin,Glazarova, Riha, Neval, Tyl and others. He liked the drama, passion and contrast between poetic and robust humour. There is a lyrical poetry in his pictures, and his roots in the cultural and popular Czech tradition constantly make themselves felt. In many of the books he used beautifully illustrated initials as an extra appetiser.

Trnka wanted to make the illustrations an intergral part of the work, to turn pictures into an organic whole with the text and thereby stimulate children's imagination. In general, straightforward children's books have always given me an impression of superficiality, since in general they appear only as inci-dental to the author's serious work. I have never adopted this way of working. All the illustrations I have done for children's books have been a definite work-ing goal for me and I have invested everything in them that I had to give.

He was non-dogmatic and innovative with his childlike illustrations for the picture books about the disobedient and wilful bear cub Micky Tubby(Misa kulicka) from the late thirties. The child's universe reappears in his poetic illustrations for Hrubin's fairy tale *Roselil* and the *Winter Witch* and for his own *The Enchanted Gate*, a comic tale of five boys playing a game in the garden behind a magic gate, with a mad tom-cat, five wild elephants, and a whale that reads and speaks Arabic. He also expressively illustrated Prokofiev's musical story *Peter and the Wolf*.

Trnka loved fairy tales and possibly reached his apogee in his many fairy tale illustrations, which display his artistic urge. For Andersen's tales he com-bined childlike simplicity with classical refinement and theatrical effects, demonstrating an entirely individual attitude to colour; the Grimm illustra-tions are supported by a folkloric style of humour, while *The Thousand and One Nights* has powerful colour pictures and beautiful Persian-style pat-terns.

莫里斯桑達克
MAURICE SENDAK

美國 UNITED STATES

1970

2013年6月10日，Google首頁以莫里斯桑達克(1928-2012)為主題，紀念他的85歲冥誕，桑達克長銷半世紀、售出近兩千萬本的代表作《野獸國》(Where the Wild Things Are)，已成為全球無數兒童的共同回憶。

桑達克1970年獲頒國際安徒生大獎，迄今都還是唯一獲此殊榮的美國插畫家。他曾五度獲得美國圖書最高榮譽「凱迪克獎」(Caldecott Medal)，國際第二大兒童文學獎項—瑞典「林格倫紀念獎」(The Astrid Lindgren Memorial Award)也於2003年將第一屆桂冠頒給桑達克。2012年5月8日，桑達克走完83年的精采一生，紐約時報寫道：「莫里斯桑達克被公認是20世紀最重要的童書藝術家，他使繪本走出一個安全無垢的世界，並將其投入一個黑暗、令人驚嚇卻又難以忘懷的美麗心靈境界。」

1963年《野獸國》、1970年《廚房之夜狂想曲》(In the Night Kitchen)、1981年《在那遙遠的地方》(Outside Over There)，跨越數十年的三部代表作，桑達克稱之為他的「繪本三部曲」，濃縮了他的生命精華，也是他回到原初起點，對「內在小孩」的一系列探討。

桑達克的內在小孩，有著悲慘的童年。雙親是猶太裔的波蘭移民，雖遷至美國紐約布魯克林，仍籠罩著二次大戰大屠殺的陰影；桑達克自小體弱多病，面對死亡的恐懼、母親無盡的眼淚和躁鬱，這些負面記憶都構築了桑達克性格中的陰暗面。

躺在病床上無法外出時，桑達克只能望向窗外畫下觀察的事物，雖不能像他所羨慕的孩子盡情玩耍、溜冰，桑達克9歲就開始創作生涯，12歲看了迪士尼音樂動畫《幻想曲》就決定要當插畫家，1937年開始寫作，1947如願成為童書繪本創作。

深知「小朋友很願意面對那些大人認為他們不該知道的模糊地帶」，桑達克的繪本創作反映出孩子在成長過程中種種焦慮、不安、恐懼、憤怒、挫折、忌妒等複雜情緒，在當時堪稱顛覆性的革命，「繪本三部曲」起初毀譽參半，《野獸國》一度是圖書館禁書，後來卻被改編成動畫、音樂劇、電影，成為備受推崇的經典。

「小朋友需要透過幻想故事來宣洩情感。這是讓他們馴服『野獸』的最佳方式。」桑達克探索孩子真實的內在世界，將負面情緒加以掌控、釋懷，轉化為溫馨的故事，令小朋友格外有共鳴。

Maurice Sendak was born in Brooklyn in 1928, the son of Polish-Jewish immigrant parents and so received his inspiration from the dual inheritance of the Jewish story-telling tradition and life in New York in the 1930s. Disney with Mickey Mouse, Chaplin, Laurel and Hardy were an enchanted world which, together with the German illustrative art of such essentially different artists as Durer and Wilhelm Busch as well as the artwork of William Blake, Cruikshank and Caldecott, are among those that he counts as his inspirers and models.

"My wish is to combine – in words and pictures, faithfully and fantas-tically – my weird, Old Country-New Country childhood...Most of all, the mystery – that is a cherished goal...Children are willing to deal with many dubious subjects that grown-ups think they shouldn't know about." Magic, fantasy, dream and play are indissolubly linked with Maurice Sendak's works.

His output is varied and extensive and includes illustrated books, books that he has written and illustrated, comic strips, pop-up books, mechanical toys, animated films, stage designs and costumes, record sleeves, and tele-vision production. The picture book Where the Wild Things Are has also been turned into an opera.

His picture books range from the childlike simplicity and warm security of books such as the Little Bear books, through the magical and fantastic world of play, as in A Sign on Rosie's Door, to the wildly imaginative and at times almost surreal universe of Where the Wild Thinigs Are and In the Night Kitchen.

He sees himself as " the interpretive illustrator". Simply reproducing the story in pictures is not enough. The pictures must reflect the soul of the text. they must expand and transform it, so that the reader's eyes are opened to new and different experiences of the book. His Grimm illustrations, for exam-ple, are characteristic in that he has chosen motifs that differ from the usual, simply to underline the depth and ambiguity of the fairy tales.

His insight into children's inner lives has made him an enthusiastic par-ticipant in the debate on the child's need to be taken seriously in art as well, despite the adult's concerns:" it is through fanrasy that children achieve catharsis. It is the best means they have for taming Wild Things.

Sendak's technical ability is astonishing and gives him the freedom to play around with all kinds of styles and pictorial forms. He composes his books as a composer constructs a piece of music, with a well-considered and refined sense of rhythm, dramatic highlights and anti-climaxes, and involve-ing all sorts of pictorial effects. He has a profound knowledge of art and provokes and challenges the adults by bringing to life children's innermost and wildest fantasies in an imaginative and artistically integrated version which unites fantasy and reality.

A succrssful picture book is a visual poem..." With his many pictorial poems, Sendak ranks today as a modern classic, and as one of the most tal-ented, original and uncompromising picture artists of the last fifty years.

Where the Wild Things Are
野獸國

史班歐森
IB SPANG OLSEN

丹麥 DENMARK

1972

2012年1月15日，史班歐森(1921-2012)以90高齡辭世，丹麥媒體以「這一天，圖畫死了」(The day the graphics died)致哀。

生於安徒生的故鄉，童話大國丹麥的哥本哈根，史班歐森是第一位獲得國際安徒生大獎桂冠的丹麥藝術家。他的去世更加凸顯他的重要性−幾乎沒有任何丹麥人，沒接觸過史班歐森的作品，長達四十餘年來，史班歐森以丹麥詩人哈夫丹的打油詩創作的《哈夫丹的ABC》(Halfdans ABC)，就是丹麥人學習字母的教材，「你為我的童年畫上色彩」是丹麥人送給史班歐森的人生註腳。

素描就是他的起點，也是他偏愛的表達方式。史班歐森的一生幾乎每天都不停地畫畫，從小就喜歡用鉛筆素描日常生活，1942年正式踏入彩色的繪圖世界，為報紙、雜誌繪製時事漫畫，訓練出極其靈活幽默的筆觸以及廣泛的風格。後來，史班歐森進入哥本哈根藝術學院學習，並曾經在一處學校擔任老師。

他的根在丹麥：丹麥的地形、風土和房子、動物、兒童、以及丹麥的民間信仰。他為安徒生童話精心打造了角色吃重的插畫，在這些知名的丹麥童話中織進幽默的底調。《天神索爾》(Guden Thor)中，高高在上的北歐天神暴躁又有點天真，眾神和他們的妻子演繹出辛辣又人性化的故事；史班歐森自編自繪的怪誕故事《沼澤姥姥的釀坊》(The Marsh Crone's Brew)，高大醜陋的姥姥像在煉巫婆湯似的，在大鍋中放入月光、夕陽餘暉、雞啼聲、夜露、狐狸耳朵、螞蝗的黏液……，沼澤地的男孩、女孩、鬼火都來幫忙，空氣中散發著丹麥夏日躁動不安的氣息。

史班歐森認為，遊戲和想像力能讓現實長出翅膀、打破界線。他的作品充滿對生命的熱愛與幽默感，富有想像力與啟發性的教育寓意，經常也運用特殊的構圖或開本來強化視覺效果。《跳不停的小紅球》(The Red Ball)在許多角落都出現小紅球，以凸顯小紅球的橫衝直撞；《月光男孩》(The Boy In the Moon)則以縱向的長幅版，表現男孩由天上緩緩降落到地面的垂直空間，而月光男孩到地面、到水下幫月亮尋找另一個月亮的任務，實則是月亮重新認識自我的旅程。

1972年，史班歐森獲頒國際安徒生大獎，此外他也獲獎無數，丹麥對這位國寶級藝術家極為禮遇，1982至1990年間，他擔任丹麥文化部童書文化委員會委員，同時活躍於丹麥皇家藝術院的學術評議會，地位相當崇高。

Artist of the country of childhood! Ib Spang Olsen can be described as briefly as that. His point of departure and preferred means of expression is his drawing, which he may subsequently color. He is a masterly draughts-man. His drawings are sensually filled with experiences and details that you can smell, feel and taste. There is an appetite for life and voracious exuber-ance and humour in them, a pleasure in the very fact of creating and a delight in exploration, but also a sensitivity to what is close and vulnerable.

He was born in 1921 and spent a childhood in Copenhagen full of adventures in the parks and back gardens – a childhood which left many traces on his later work. He trained as a teacher and later as a graphic artist and painter. His production ranges widely, from book illustrations to works he himself wrote and illustrated, from catoons to posters, films theatre and television.

Ib Spang Olsen combines the fabulous and imaginative with the instructive and enlightening. He shares the child's curiosity,thirst for knowledge and capac-ity for wonder, and he willingly shares his own knowledge and imagination.

His roots are in Denmark: Danish landscapes, background and houses, Danish animals, Danish children, Danish folk beliefs. In his carefully com-posed and vital illustrations for Hans Christian Andersen's fairy tales Spang Olsen has woven in humorous undertones from well-known Danish motifs. *In Mosekonens bryg(The Marsh Crone's Brew)* he captures nature's magic in the most wonderful way; there is the hum of a Danish summer when the robust Marshcrone is brewing her beer,while the marsh-girls and boys and will-o'the-wisps lend a hand. The stories about the violent, ruddy and high-living, but also somewhat naïve Norse gods and their sensual and buxom wives *(Guden Thor)* have found in Spang Olsen an interpreter who does full justice to the racy stories.

A uniquely congenial partnership has existed for a lifetime between Spang Olsen and the poet Halfdan Rasmussen. Know and loved by every Danish child, their rhynes and pictures constitute a whole, to the extent that one cannot be thought of without the other. Spang Olsen's baroque humour and comical fancies, poetic imagination and sparkling vitality add new dimensions to the verses.

With the story *Drengen I manen*, where the boy in the moon is sent to earth to fetch the moon that the man in the moon can see in a alke, Spang Olsen has created one of the most delightful picture books, where he can revel in the poetic realism so characteristic of his work.

Spang Olsen's art is timeless: he belongs to the classical genre of draw-ing and illustration that is outside time and place, while at the same time capturing and sensing the spirit of the period. For him, artist and pedagogue go hand in hand; fantasy, play and imagination lend wings to reality and burst its bounds. ''What is such fun about what we call the fantastic in thecon-text of children's books is that the child knows how it would have behaved and therefore enjoys crossing the boundaries. It is testing the limits that always gives pleasure.''

Nails are for nailing
and feet are for feeting
hats are for hatting
and trumpets for trumping
dogs are for dogging
and parents for pairing
beds are for bedding
and pants are for panting
boots are for booting
and bottoms for botting
beasts are for having a chat on
while potties are built to be sat on.

In Do-Not-Land we may not do
all kinds of do-not things,
do not toot or toodle-oo,
do not swim or swing on swings.
Do not narkle. Do not flortle.
Do not sparkle. Do not chortle.
See the pointing Do-Not hand?
That's for those in Do-Not-Land.

In You-May-Land it's you may that
and you may this as well,
you may fight or fall down flat,
you may joke or jump or yell.
You may climb, or play in mud.
Laugh. Rhyme. Thwack! Thud!
Not a single thing is banned
in yippee yahoo You-May-Land.

Hokus Pokus
戲法

The Marsh Crone's Brew
沼澤姥姥的釀坊

The Marsh Crone's Brew
沼澤姥姥的釀坊

梅斯伽利
FARSHID MESGHALI

伊朗　IRAN

1974

國際安徒生大獎於1974年將插畫桂冠頒贈第一位亞洲創作者，得主是當時年僅31歲的伊朗藝術家梅斯伽利(1943-)，相當令人意外; 伊朗的童書插畫、繪本在國際間的表現，至今仍然具有強勁力道，主要得力於1960年代就已打下培育創作人才的紮實基礎。

梅斯伽利1943年生於伊斯法罕，早在1964年他還就讀德黑蘭大學藝術系時，就已開始和《Negin Magazine》合作，踏上職業平面設計師、插畫家之路。畢業後，他在1968年進入德黑蘭的「兒童及青少年智力發展協會」(Institute for the Intellectual Development of Children and Young Adults)，首次為童書畫插畫、製作兒童動畫電影。

今日伊朗有許多動人的電影經典之作，尤其兒童主題最為出色，「兒童及青少年智力發展協會」居功厥偉。當時的時代背景是: 1953年重新上台的伊朗國王巴勒維二世，於1963年開始推動「白色革命」實行多項社會改革，在巴勒維王后的提議之下，「兒童及青少年智力發展協會」創辦於1965年，並於1969年聘請伊朗電影導演阿巴斯(Abbas Kiarostami)成立電影分部，帶動了1970年代的伊朗電影新浪潮運動。

阿巴斯被尊為伊朗兒童電影大師，生於1941年的他，與梅斯伽利是同一世代，也都是被延攬到「兒童及青少年智力發展協會」的藝文菁英。由於有這個機構作為保護傘，巴勒維國王的獨裁統治，難能可貴的有了一處自由呼吸的創作樂土，也培育出許多伊朗童書插畫、繪本、兒童電影的優秀人才。

梅斯伽利為此機構創作出多部獲獎的動畫片、電影海報、童書插畫，分別與多位伊朗作家合作的插畫代表作有1968年《小黑魚》(The Little Black Fish)、1970年《詹姆希德王》(Jamshid King)、1973年《藍眼睛的男孩》(The Blue-Eyed Boy)等。

這些作品或取材自古波斯神話，或當代創作童書，多被視為具有弦外之音的政治寓言; 梅斯伽利的圖像融合插畫藝術與民俗傳統元素，甚至創造新的波斯文字書寫法，構築出獨樹一幟的現代伊朗繪本風格，

「1979革命」迎來伊斯蘭宗教領袖柯梅尼的神權統治，不僅巴勒維國王流亡海外，新的政治打壓也迫使大批伊朗電影人、文化人出走。梅斯伽利也在1979年移居巴黎，繼而在1984年搬到美國南加州，在歐美期間，梅斯伽利轉而投入油畫、雕塑以及數位藝術創作，並曾舉辦多次展覽。

1998年，他回到伊朗擔任藝術顧問，協助規劃重量級的系列叢書《伊朗兒童文學史》(The History of Children's Literature in Iran)，前兩冊於2001年問世。目前他定居於德黑蘭的工作室，創作雕塑與裝置藝術。

Farshid Mesghali was born in 1943 in Isfahan. While studying arts at Tehran University, he began his professional career as a graphic designer and illustrator with *Negin Magazine* in 1964. After graduation, he joined the Institute for the Intellectual Development of Children and Young Adults in Tehran, in 1968, illustrating books for children and creating animated films for children for the first time. During the years 1970 to 1978 he made many of his award-winning animated films, posters for films and illustrations of children's books for this Institute. In 1979 he moved to Paris. For the next four years he worked as an artist, producing a number of paintings as well as sculptures.

In 1986 he moved to Southern California, where he opened a graphic design studio. In1994 he started to work for a multi-media company in San Francisco, producing and designing virtual reality environments for the Internet. In 1988 he returned to Iran, where he is art advisor to a multi-volume monumental work entitled *The History of Children's Literature in Iran*, the first two volumes of which appeared in 2001.

Mesghali was the first winner of the Hans Children Andersen Award from Asia. He is one of the elite in modern Iranian picture-book art, and has influenced several generations of younger colleagues. He mainly produces pictures for exiting Persian fairy tales, combining elements of modern illustrative art with elements of the folklore tradition. Among other things, this is expressed in the framing of pictures, the use of ornaments, and some stylisation of the figures. He has also created new ways of writing the Persian alphabet.

In *Mahi-ye siyahe Koochooloo (The little black fish)* grandmother tells her twelve thousand grandchildren the story of the little black fish who left home to discover the world. He reaches his goal – the sea – because he has both courage and fortitude. The book shows the importance of learning from personal experience, the first against prejudice and for freedom and individual rights.

Pesarak-e cheshm aabi (The Blue-Eyes Boy) is the story of a little village boy who sees everything in blue. He does not want to be different and is taken with much hope to old Zacharia in another village for a cure. The operation ends tragically, for when the little boy opens his eyes the world is black. In this book, where the pictures are inspired by pop art, several different techniques are used. Each spread constitutes a whole into which the typography is woven as part of the graphic expression.

While Mesghali's work is rooted in his culture, his childhood and his special experience, his themes and visual language are universal and can be understood worldwide.

The King Jamshid
詹姆士德國王

The Little Black Fish
小黑魚

The City of Snakes
蛇城

Me, My Doll and the Hedgehog
我，我的娃娃和刺蝟

塔提雅娜瑪芙琳娜
TATJANA MAWRINA

俄羅斯　RUSSIA

1976

塔提雅娜瑪芙琳娜(1900-1996)是國際安徒生大獎史上唯一的俄羅斯插畫家得主，她97年的長壽一生橫跨沙皇帝俄、蘇聯、俄羅斯聯邦等三大政體，祖國悠遠的歷史、豐厚的文化、驚濤駭浪的時代，交織成瑪芙琳娜從民俗藝術提煉養分，充滿鮮活生命力的繪本圖像。

瑪芙琳娜出生於窩瓦河畔的下諾夫哥羅德(Nizhny Novgorod)，城市名稱曾在1932至1990年間更名為「高爾基」(Gorky)，以紀念生於當地的俄國文豪高爾基。

這座13世紀的古城，古蹟名勝眾多，尤以「下諾夫哥羅德的克里姆林宮」著稱。當地的俄羅斯民間藝術傳統色彩濃厚，瑪芙琳娜自小就留下深刻印象，並在日後深刻反映在她的創作上。

1917年俄國革命帶來翻天覆地的巨變，推翻帝俄建立蘇維埃政權，在動盪不安的後革命時期，瑪芙琳娜於1920年代接受藝術教育，一度曾加入前衛藝術　運動「十三人團」(Thirteen Group)，並以「塔提雅娜莉貝迪娃」(Tatjana Lebedeva)之名參與1929年的首次聯展。

二戰期間，她深受俄羅斯民俗版畫「魯波克」(Lubok)的形象生動、色彩鮮麗所吸引，隨後在1940至50年代，走訪俄國各地采風、蒐集古老聖像與民間藝術，結合傳統元素與西歐現代繪畫手法，創作出一系列獨具個人風格的圖畫。

「我的小城故事系列、風景素描、人物肖像、花卉畫都不是獨立存在的。」瑪芙琳娜於1977年出版的德文版回憶錄《窩瓦河與北德維納河之間》(Between Volga and Dwina)寫道：「對我來說，它們是童話插畫的入門研究。它們來自我流浪、旅行路上所見的一切，還有我在漫長人生中所閱讀、經歷的一切。」

瑪芙琳娜畢生創作的童書插畫多達兩百餘本，其中不少取材自俄國著名詩人普金希作品，為童話詩《死公主和七勇士》、《漁夫與金魚的故事》以及浪漫詩《盧斯蘭與魯密拉》繪製插畫。1965年《神奇動物》(Fabulous Beasts)、1969年《童話 ABC》(Fairy Tale ABC)等作品，則都是瑪芙琳娜的原創繪本，超美的大膽配色、具有裝飾趣味的視覺元素、極富玩心的幽默感，都讓她的圖畫變得更令人驚艷。

1976年，國際安徒生大獎桂冠頒予瑪芙琳娜;1991年蘇聯解體，瑪芙琳娜仍然長青;甚至1996年她的精采一生結束之後，瑪芙琳娜的繪本依舊魅力四射。

Tatjana Mawrina (1902-1997) was born in the ancient Volga city of Nizhny Novgorod. This city and its suburbs, rich with the traditions of Russian folk art, made a strong impression on the little girl, which was later reflected in her creative activities. She received her artistic education in the stormy post-revolutionary years, during the first decade of the Soviet regime. Besides painting, the young artist was also greatly interested in book illustration, but it took her a few decades to find her own images, her own colorful style.

During the years of World War II she addressed herself for the first time to the monuments of ancient Russian culture. In the forties and fifties Mawrina travelled widely through her native land and created a series of pictures, in which she depicted ancient Russian towns, their architecture and the surrounding landscapes.

In Mawrina's illustrations one can sense various echoes of ancient Russian art. Her illustrations at times resemble traditional toys, wood carvings, treacle cakes, at other times, tiles or book miniatures, sometimes all these mingled together in a single work. Mawrina successfully embraced a great number of folk art traditions in her work, and her thorough knowledge of these traditions enabled her to enhance the poetic essence of motifs used in visual and oral folklore. She subordinated these vivid traditions to the demands of contemporary book illustration, enriching her pictures with the brilliant colours - red and green, yellow and blue and the bold lines of early twentieth century painting. Her books are beautifully designed from beginning to end, abounding with various decorative elements: ornaments, headpieces, tailpieces, calligraphy.

Mawrina's illustrations to well-known Russian folk and fairy tales include popular tales and poems by A.S. Pushkin. Her characters, be they human or animals, are always depicted with warmth and humour. One of the most striking works by Mawrina is her *Fairy Tale ABC Book* which may serve as an original encyclopedia of all her book art. Here we meet the images from fairy tales she has illustrated and see the main features of her ornamental style.

"My town cycles and landscape sketches, the portraits and flower pieces none of them claims to stand alone. For me they are rather preliminary studies for the fairy tale illustrations. They are the outcome of everything I have seen on my wanderings and travels, and everything I have read and experienced in my long life." (From the German edition of her memoirs: *Zwischen Wolga und Dwina (Between Volga and Dwina*. Leipzig, 1977)

Fabulous beasts
神奇動物

斯凡歐特
SVEND OTTO

丹麥 DENMARK

1978

斯凡歐特 (1916-1996) 的畫作有一種清新的氣息,透明水彩的層次豐富微妙,一如北歐國度的冷冽空氣,迎著森林中的霧氣或暖陽,透出乾淨的光,寫實場景也發散著空靈的藝術性,難怪他常被稱作「斯堪地那維亞的自然主義者」(Scandinavian naturalist)。

2016年6月2 日適逢斯凡歐特百歲冥誕,歐洲現役最古老的天文台–丹麥哥本哈根圓塔 (Rundetaarn),今年春天推出一項斯凡歐特紀念展「圖像的説書人–童話或現實」(Poctorial Storyteller- Fairytale and Reality),由斯凡歐特的家人提供許多珍貴作品,呈現他無論童話插圖、自然寫生風景都爐火純青的繪畫造詣。

歐凡斯特1916年生於哥本哈根,白小就喜歡畫畫,1930年代他在丹麥修讀 藝校的夜間課程之後,1938年進入倫敦的聖馬丁藝術學院深造。

1968年為安徒生童話《樅樹》(The Fir Tree)繪製插畫,是斯凡歐特的第一部繪本,此後,他曾繪製《拇指姑娘》、《醜小鴨》等眾多膾炙人口的安徒生童話,集結為《孩子們的安徒生童話》(The children's Andersen),斯凡歐特捕捉這些故事神髓,畫出或詩意、或神秘感、或憂鬱、悲傷或幽默的動人場景。他重視細節、用愛描繪丹麥風光、理解孩子對魔法世界的好奇探索,總能把奇幻變得真實,滿足每個小朋友的童話之夢。

倘徉於安徒生童話世界之外,《睡美人》、《穿長靴的貓》等格林童話、歐洲童話,也在斯凡歐特筆下構成足以與迪士尼分庭抗禮的圖像風格。狄更斯、湯瑪斯曼、林格倫等眾多大師經典,也常是斯凡歐特創作取材的養分。

斯凡歐特的畢生創作,至少有50餘本童書都是再創造的故事,他以繪畫的力量重新詮釋,成功將眾多經典都轉化成斯凡歐特風格的作品,呼應了1978年他獲頒安徒生大獎時,吐露心中的祈願:「當你坐在書房裡,試著把文字加進圖畫中,你想把充滿想法和情感的畫送給全世界,你希望能得到回應,希望這些圖畫也能在別人心中激起相似的想法和情感…」

精準、確實、敍事時的喜悅一這些全都是大量的準備工作和徹底研究的結果。水彩大師斯凡歐特,在忠於故事的氣氛和年代的插畫中,強化文字的訊息,反映了生活、情感及對社會的了解,「圖像的説書人」確實將童話與現實的藝術三昧,都揮灑得淋漓盡致。

Svend Otto (Srensen) (1916-1996) began drawing as a child and at an early age tended evening classes at the Danish School of Design. Later on he went to an art school in Copenhagen and in London. A children's book cover finally gave rise to an avalance of commissions, and for the rest of his life he remained one of Denmark's most sought-after illustrators and children's book creators.

With his illustrations to *Bornenens H.C. Andersen (The children's Andersen)* , a collection of the writer's most child-oriented fairy tales, Svend Otto captured the many facets of these tales: their poetry and mystery, their melancholy sadness and humour. His loving attention to detail, his depictions of the Danish landscape and his understanding of the child's fascination for the magic reality of the world of fairy tale make these illustrations special.

It was no accident that *Grantraeet (The fir tree)* by Andersen was his first picture book. He loved woods and trees, he was a naturalist who had to experience and see what he drew: trees, seasons, weather, children's and animals' movements. Among the fairy tale characters, the troll is one of his favourites: cheerful and good-humoured, malicious and coy, shrewd and cunning, and always with a trick up his sleeve. Trolls and trees – fairy tale and reality. Svend Otto wanted to make everyday things fantastic and fantastic things realistic. Generally harmonious, cheerful and poetic, his pictures fulfil every child's dreams of fairy tales.

Precision, authenticity and the joy of storytelling are all the result of a great deal of preparatory work and thorough research. Svend Otto generally used watercolour, a technique of which he was a master. The use of the colour grey is characteristic of him, though eventually he would also employ the whole palette. Faithful to the atmosphere and period of the stories, sympathetic to the message of the text, his pictures reflect life and feelings, as well as social understanding. This is evident, for instance, in the illustrations for the festive Danish Christmas song Sikken voldsom traengsel og alarm (What a crowd and what a noise), where he depicts the bourgeoisie's brilliant Christmas feast, contrasting with the poor who simply stand and stare as onlookers.

Svend Otto's work can be divided between fairy tale illustrations - especially Andersen and Grimm - and picture books about children in foreign countries and in the past, which he also wrote himself. His desire to show realistic aspects of life is expressed in the historical *Stormfloden (The flood)*, a story with two children as the central characters, which describes the ravages of a flood in southern Denmark in 1872, on the islands of the artist's childhood. The picture books about children in different countries have the same aim. They are exciting and informative, containing dramatic episodes and pictures with many details. His books fulfil the hope he expressed when he received the Hans Christian Andersen Award: "When you sit in your study and try to put a text into pictures, you try to send drawings full of ideas and emotions out into the world, and you hope for a response the hope that these pictures will arouse similar ideas and emotions in others..."

Grimms Märchen
格林童話

赤羽末吉
SUEKICHI AKABA

日本　JAPAN

1980

1980年國際安徒生大獎的插畫桂冠，首度頒予日本，自學成家的插畫家赤羽末吉 (1910-1990)獲此殊榮，到底厲害在哪裡？日本兒童文學評論家鳥越信的評析，精準勾勒出赤羽末吉的成就–讓日本畫的手法在現代的圖畫書中得到再生，讓民間故事在現代得以復甦。

赤羽末吉1910年生於東京，1931年移民到滿洲國，在中國東北度過15年的青壯時期，當時在工廠工作的赤羽末吉，利用閒暇時間畫畫，完全無師自通。1939年他把自己的畫作寄到全國藝術展覽會，接連三次得獎。他在1947年回到日本，先當了一陣子的自由工作者，然後在東京的美國大使館公關部服務20年。

直到半百之齡，赤羽才開始嘗試繪本創作。他在49歲那年遇到「日本圖書書之父」松居直，松居直看了赤羽的畫稿之後，問他想畫什麼樣的書？赤羽不假思索回答：「我想畫雪國。」

1961年，50歲的赤羽出版他的第一本繪本《斗笠地藏》，以水墨渲染畫出這則發生在雪國的日本民間故事。這本書讓他完成長久以來的夢想：用水墨技法來畫繪本。以往書畫界大多認為小朋友喜歡明亮的色彩，幾乎不會採用黑白色調 的水墨，但這項大膽嘗試卻廣受雪國兒童的喜愛。

此後，赤羽末吉的作品如《鶴妻》、《雪女》也都取材自日本民間怪譚，再加上《傳統鬼怪繪本》系列，為赤羽末吉贏得「鬼之赤羽」稱號。

赤羽的插畫深受日本傳統繪畫影響，以多種層次灰色調作畫的瑞士插畫家霍夫曼 (Felix Hoffmann)也對他的風格帶來影響。赤羽對日本傳統服飾的熟稔與豐富知識，以及他曾擔任舞台劇服裝設計的經歷，都極有助於他創作古典題材的細節刻畫。

為了貼近故事，他在紙張、畫筆、媒材、色彩，都挑剔得近乎完美主義，赤羽末吉代表作《馬頭琴》就是經典佳例。當時。赤羽完成《斗笠地藏》之後又找上松居直，問他：「您見過360度地平線的風景嗎？」赤羽想表現在蒙古大草原見過天蒼蒼野茫茫的塞外風光，1961年出版的16開本圖畫書，卻和理想有一大段差距。

幾年之後，松居直和赤羽末吉彌補了遺憾–由於《馬頭琴》原稿毀於一場火災，赤羽重新繪製脫胎換骨的《馬頭琴》，1967年問世就帶來強烈衝擊–畫作由9張增至23張，橫開本的水平展開，鋪陳了廣闊無垠草原上，少年蘇和被強奪心愛的白馬，白馬死了之後化為馬頭琴的淒美傳說;這本書在日本暢銷逾百萬冊，也樹立了赤羽末吉創作生涯最重要的里程碑。

Suekichi Akaba (1910-1990) was born in Tokyo. In 1931 he emigrated to Manchuria, where he lived for fifteen years. While there, he worked industry but also painted in his spare time. In 1939 he sent his picture to the National Art Exhibition where he subsequently won special recognition three times. After returning to Japan in 1947, he first freelanced and then worked for twenty years in the Public Relations Office of the American Embassy in Tokyo.

Akaba was self-taught, except for about one year's apprenticeship with a painter at the beginning of his career. He never had a teacher, having mastered the techniques of traditional painting by himself - though it considered to be a most difficult process without instruction.

Akaba was fifty when, in 1961, he created his first picture book, *Kasa Jizo (Roku Jizo and the hats)*, based on an old folk tale, as are all his following picture books. Here he realized an old dream: to illustrate a picture book in Indian ink, a technique which had not previously been used in picture books, on the assumption that children prefer bright colours. The story is set in the snowy winter so typical of Japan, which made it especially popular among children in areas with a lot of snow.

As an illustrator, Akaba was strongly influenced by traditional Japanese painting - his entire work represents a natural continuation of native traditions. The second strand traceable in his art reflects the influence of the illustrator Felix Hoffmann. Akaba's style reveals an intimate knowledge of traditional garments. He actually worked as a costume designer for the stage. This is of no small significance, since in Japanese theatre costumes function as an important expressive device.

In his illustrations Akaba used many different kinds of Japanese paper, each fulfilling a specific function, communicating specific moods or generally mediating expression. Akaba's unabating interest in Japanese paper, including manufacturing techniques, is not surprising considering that paper is the material he mostly used as his medium of expression. His collages using different kinds of paper in combination with drawing and painting bear his hallmark of technical perfection and elicit a powerful emotional response in the child.

The year 1972 marked a turning point in Akaba's work. He began to move away from soft brush drawings, preferring more definitive contours The brighter colours he chose for composition give his pictures space and a certain lightness of movement.

Akaba's accurate depiction of his characters, whether they are people or animals, his division of the action into scenes, the way he tells his story alternating between movement and stillness towards the climax, and his humour that is built on centuries-old Japanese tradition - all of these represent a high point in the art of the modern Japanese pictures book.

Suekichi Akaba, From *Suho's White Horse*, 1967
馬頭琴

Suekichi Akaba, From *Suho's White Horse*, 1967
馬頭琴

Suekichi Akaba, From *Fly Away, Birdies!*, 1978
快逃，小鳥們

Suekichi Akaba, From *Oniroku and the Carpenter*, 1962
木匠與鬼六

澤比紐里科利齊
ZBIGNIEW RYCHLICKI

波蘭 POLAND

1982

「武力衝突、缺乏包容、社會不公、種族歧視，它們是社會的病灶，孩子們也深受其害。」波蘭插畫家澤比紐里科利齊 (1922-1989) 獲頒1982年國際安徒生大獎時，有感而發：「現在的孩子必須在毫無防備的情況下，面對世界上各種戲劇性的事件，從過去到現在，他們的問題一直都是我最關心的議題。我不斷在我的作品中強調：藝術在小朋友長大成人的過程中，扮演了很特別的角色。我也強調藝術在創意上的貢獻讓美好理想得以實現：孩子有權得到快樂的童年！」

里科利齊1922年生於波蘭東南部一處村落，自波蘭第二大城克拉科夫的藝術學院畢業後，他於1949年遷居華沙，任職波蘭歷史最悠久的童書出版社「我們的書店」(Nasza Księgarnia)30餘年，從藝術編輯一路做到副社長，畢生創作過的童書多達150餘本，並曾贏得世界各地小朋友遴選、波蘭國家頒發的「微笑勳章騎士」(Knight of the Order of Smile)。

里科利齊深信，童書應該要有道德觀和社會價值觀，透過插畫讓小讀者更加瞭解真實世界的生活，培養他們對社會的參與感。

他將插畫視為和繪畫、平面藝術等量齊觀的創意領域，融合波蘭民間藝術、版畫、拼貼等各式當代藝術技法，創作出具有著抒情色調、創新精神的迷人圖像，對當代波蘭插畫產生深遠的重大影響。

里科利齊最具代表性的作品，首推波蘭人的頭號兒時玩伴--「垂耳熊」(Miś Uszatek)，數十年來，只要一想到這隻波蘭最受歡迎的泰迪熊，波蘭人腦中就會響起卡通結束時播放的晚安曲：「上床的時間到囉~月兒已經高高掛天上，小朋友們愛熊熊，熊熊也愛小朋友…」

這隻波蘭熊的耳朵不對稱，左耳軟趴趴垂著，所以名叫「垂耳熊」。波蘭童書作家揚克札斯基(Czeslaw Janczarski)於1957年創辦兒童雙周刊《熊》(Miś)，同時由他勾勒初稿，里科利齊完成視覺圖像的方式，一起創造出可愛的「垂耳熊」作為吉祥物，發表在雜誌創刊號，一砲而紅。

「垂耳熊」自1975年成為帶狀電視卡通主角，同時發展一系列童書繪本，溫暖友善的「垂耳熊」是每個波蘭小朋友床邊故事的最愛，也成為一代代波蘭人成長歲月的共同回憶。

2014年波蘭一處中部小鎮否決「小熊維尼」成為遊樂園吉祥物，小鎮要員說這隻迪士尼小熊「衣著不整、性別不明、不男不女」，並用波蘭的「垂耳熊」「全身都穿著衣服，整整齊齊」作為對照。消息傳出，雖被引為趣談，卻也凸顯出里科利齊創造的波蘭熊，確實贏得波蘭大眾的衷心愛戴！

Zbigniew Rychlicki (1922-1989), painter, graphic artist and illustrator, was born in Orzechowka, Poland. He was a graduate of the Academy of Fine Arts in Cracow. He served as art editor, head of the art section and vice director of the State children's book publishing house Nasza ksiegarnia in Warsaw.

Rychlicki's artistic creed rests on the conviction that children's books should possess moral and social values. Illustration should provide a guide to real life and foster a sense of social involvement in children and young people. Through his creative approach to the function of illustration, his work continues to exercise a major influence on the development of contemporary Polish illustration. Rychlicki explored new demanding forms of illustration and envisaged illustration as a field of creativity indissolubly linked with painting and national and international graphic art. Fascinated by the creative process of illustration, he believed that visual perception should promote the child's creative thought and action.

Rychlicki's art is characterized by compositions of lyrical colour and a probing for new forms, as well as an inclination for the grotesque. He created outstanding illustrations to Polish folk tales and songs, making use of elements from the rich source of his country's folk art. His fairy tale illustrations include masterful depictions of local settings and fanciful, imaginative characters. In addition to his folkloristic picture books Rychlicki also illustrated nonsense verse, popular nonfiction and contemporary classics such as *The Wizard of Oz*. Today, he is best known as the creator, with the author Czeslaw Janczarski, of the popular figure of Mis Uszatek, the lopsided teddy bear.

The decorative quality and original stylization characteristic of Rychlicki's illustrations never detract from the communicative power of the underlying message. Illustration - as he saw it - can never be reduced to a mechanical transcript of a literary scene or situation. Just as a composer employs tones to express emotions, the illustrator creates a work of graphic art on a set literary theme - an artefact functioning across the boundaries of literary subject matter.

"The problems of the child, defenceless in the face of the dramas of today's world, have been and continue to be of the utmost importance to me. In my work I have constantly stressed the very special role of art in the shaping of young characters. I have stressed the creative contribution to the realisation of the beautiful ideal - the right to a happy childhood. Armed conflicts, intolerance, social injustice and racial discrimination are now among the sources of those terrible maladies whose effects on society do not exclude children." (From his Hans Christian Andersen Award acceptance speech).

Teddy Puschelohrs Neue Freunde
米斯雅和朋友們

Klechdy domowe
童話故事集

Not far from Rzeszów
克拉科夫的不遠處

Not far from Rzeszów
克拉科夫的不遠處

安野光雅
MITSUMASA ANNO

日本　JAPAN

1984

「安野光雅(1926-　)在促進東西方的藝術交流與相互瞭解方面，扮演了日益重要的角色。」國際安徒生大獎評審團如此稱譽1984年得主：「他的創作極富傳奇性，卻能吸引各國欣賞者普遍的共鳴和喜愛，是一個具有驚人才華的知性藝術家。他的圖畫書不但十分優美，且具有極高的科學概念。」

1926年生於日本島根縣的山中小鎮津和野，家中經營旅館，安野一直很渴望能去「山的另一頭」看看，「旅行」日後成為他童書創作的重要主軸，也形成他不斷探索世界的生活態度。

雖然自小就以繪畫為志業，也曾經舉辦個人畫展，安野光雅直到42歲，才出版人生中第一本圖畫書《奇妙國》。在此之前，他曾擔任小學老師長達18年，為他開啟繪本創作之路的伯樂，是學生家長松居直，也正是發掘赤羽末吉的才華，被譽為「日本圖畫書之父」的「福音館」出版社老闆。

1968年，安野光雅處女作《奇妙國》問世，如同荷蘭畫家艾雪(M. C. Escher)展現魔幻空間錯覺趣味，激發想像力、卻幾乎沒什麼文字的繪本，令松居直暗自不安；果然，這本書起初在日本未受重視，只有數學家和科學家覺得有意思，反倒是1970年在美國獲獎，成功打開國際市場，才又紅回日本。

安野後來推出更為複雜的繪本，《ABC之書》、《五十音》等都以童心來重新展現視覺設計構成之美。不過，安野最感興趣的題材仍在於「人」，將生活經驗和生命歷練融入創作，展現溫暖、感性、細膩的動人之美，他的《旅之繪本》系列自1977年以來，陸續出版中歐、義大利、英國、美國、西班牙、丹麥、中國、日本等8冊，以橫跨近30年的時間向度，帶引讀者隨著安野精細的描繪記錄來遊歷世界，同時透視他的生命之旅、想像之旅。

這位現年90歲高齡的日本插畫大師，獲頒國際安徒生大獎桂冠之後，仍保有旺盛的生命力與創造力。曾與安野一同於1993年來台環島的作家司馬遼太郎，形容安野是「能在自我的世界保持著童心，熬過風霜、世俗與歲月，並且還能滋潤自己心田深處的童真，使其趨於桃紅的肥碩」。

2000年「安野光雅美術館」在他的故鄉津和野開幕，安野留給觀眾一段可愛的話：「請想像一下，我在畫畫的時候，一邊想著什麼呢？童心、幻想，這些都是免費的，既不會增加行李的重量，也不容易壞掉，從這座美術館回去的時候，請順道帶回去吧，說不定會是很好的土產禮物哦～」

受到安野光雅感召的人，會發現這位老先生至今仍然孜孜不倦創作，他的近作《那記憶中如神話般的時光─安野光雅水彩自繪人生》更令人深感：閱讀這位溫暖、豁達、睿智的繪本大師，整個人就是一本豐富精采的書呀！

Mitsumasa Anno is famous for highly detailed, skilful illustrations which display his love for mathematics and science as well as his appreciation of foreign culture and travel. His drawings, which are often compared to those of the Dutch graphic artist M.C. Escher, not only abound with visual trickery and illusions but also display a playful sense of humour. Many of his books contain hidden jokes and pranks which are intended to amuse and lead readers to imaginative thinking about numbers, counting, the alphabet, or complex concepts of time and space. Operating on different levels of understanding, Anno's books appeal to both children and adults.

Mitsumasa Anno was born in 1926 in Tsuwano, a small isolated community located in a valley surrounded by mountains. While growing up Anno had desire to experience places beyond these mountains - a theme very much reflected in his books for children. During World War II Anno was drafted into the army. In 1948, he received a degree from Yamaguchi Teacher Training College. Before engaging in a career in art, he taught elementary school in Tokyo for ten years.

Anno's first two picture books reflect his love of playing with visual perception. *Fushigina E. (Topsy Turvies)* in 1968 was followed by *Sakasama (Upside Downers)*. The first plays with tricks with perspective and logic while the second contains illustrations that convey different images depending on the angle or direction from which they are looked at. In presenting such illustrations, Anno hoped to stimulate the powers of young people's imaginations.

Anno's later, more complex picture books include *Anno's Alphabet* which features "impossible" woodgrain letters of the Latin alphabet that are framed within decorative borders containing objects beginning with each letter. "As a Japanese I have never felt very close to the alphabet, and it is therefore possible for me to regard the letters of the alphabet quit objectively as materials with which to design freely. I think that Europeans have a deep cultural relationship with the alphabet, and as a result find it difficult to achieve the sense of detachment from it that is easy for me. The art of lettering carries on its shoulders the weight of a long and dense history of design, and that perhaps handicaps people's ideas in some way."

In 1977 Anno published the first in a series of his acclaimed "journey" books, which recount in pictures his travels through Europe and the United States. *Anno's Journey* arose from travels Anno made to Scandinavia, Germany and England. It is a wordless book that is a mass of colourful detail, a picture narrative, and a poetic meditation in narrative form. Whithout a written text as a guide, readers are left to invent stories of their own. Through these books Anno hopes to communicate universal messages to his readers.

In addition to his picture books, Anno is also an accomplished painter and graphic artist who has displayed his work in numerous exhibitions in galleries and museums.

Anno's Journey - Italy(1978)
(「旅の絵本II」 1978年 福音館)
旅之繪本II － 義大利篇

Anno's Medieval World (1979)
(「天動説の絵本」1979年 福音館)
天動説

羅伯英潘
ROBERT INGPEN

澳大利亞　AUSTRALIA

1986

1986年在國際安徒生大獎史上極其特殊–這一年的兩位得主，文學獎得主派翠西亞瑞森(Patricia Wrightson, 1921-2010)、插畫獎得主羅伯英潘(1936-)都來自澳洲–且國際安徒生大獎的「澳洲年」奇觀絕無僅有，在他們之前、之後，再也沒有其他澳洲創作者出現在得獎名單中。

兩年之後，羅伯英潘為派翠西亞瑞森1973年小說《納岡和星星》(The Nargun and the Stars)創作的繪本於1988年出版，兩位澳洲大師攜手合作，表達他們對家園與自然環保的關懷。《納岡和星星》是澳洲第一本以原住民神話為題材的少年奇幻小說，一如瑞森曾指出「我大可寫大家較為熟悉的歐洲精靈，但我知道有一個國度跟那些幻想國度一樣神奇魔幻。澳洲就是我唯一知道的，我想寫的那個國度。」

澳大利亞的拉丁語原意是「未知的南方大陸」，四面環海的無垠大地，覆蓋著「紅色中心」的沙漠、熱帶雨林與多樣的自然景觀，自然生態環保觀念覺醒相對較早。羅伯英潘1974年創作的第一本童書插畫作品，正是澳洲童書作家柯林狄利(Colin Thiele)深富環保思想的1964年名著《暴風雨中的男孩》(Storm Boy)，敘述一名男孩和他的鵜鶘的友情。

羅伯英潘1936年生於維多利亞省的季隆(Geelong)，從當地的藝術學校畢業之後，第一份工作是為澳洲聯邦科學與工業研究組織(CSIRO)將科學調研成果繪製成圖像記錄，這段經歷訓練出敏銳觀察力、精確的寫實功力，以及如科學家般進行嚴謹考證、研究主題的精神。

在澳洲CSIRO以及為聯合國在墨西哥、秘魯從事的科學調研記錄，促使羅伯英潘關注自然議題，《我愛大自然》、《生命之歌》、《和平在人間》等書都是羅伯英潘插畫的綠色主題。此外，他也透過公共建築壁畫、設計郵票、為澳大利亞北領地設計區徽和旗幟等任務，向大眾宣導環境保護和國家文化遺產相關議題的重要性。

羅伯英潘的畫風極其細膩寫實逼真，卻又不似照片忠實再現，而是具有深厚繪畫功力，構圖、層次、場景、氛圍都富有戲劇張力，雄渾大器，流洩著古典繪畫功力的沈穩優美。

在他創作的上百本圖書書中，有不少童書名著如《小木偶》、《金銀島》、馬克吐溫《白象失竊記》等，又以歷史傳記主題最受矚目，他畫過馬可波羅、莎士比亞、德蕾莎修女、聖雄甘地甚至東方的玄奘、三國的曹操與孔明等上百位古今中外人物，都在羅伯英潘的跨文化穿梭中，神形俱足，煥發高尚的靈魂與人性光輝。

Robert Ingpen was born in Melbourne in 1936 but grew up and was educated in Geelong, Victoria. After graduation from Art School he worked as artist and illustrator for the Commonwealth scientific and Industrial Research organization and later for the United Nations in Mexico and Peru. In Australia he has painted murals for public buildings, designed postage stamps and the coat-of-arms and flag for Australia's Northern Territory. He has been actively involved in the development of tourism and recreation, and in promoting public understanding of conservation, environmental and national heritage issues.

Ingpen has been illustrating children's books since 1974. when *Storm Boy* was published. This book conveys a haunting impression of the vast and lonely Australian coastline and the profound, unsentimental relationship of lonely boy with his environment and his beloved pelican.

Many of Ingpen's subjects come from the factual, real world of history technology and science but in some books, such as his magnificent *Encyclopedia of Things That Never Were*, he combines historic facts and a lot of what he calls "whimagery" -insight into realms beyond vision.

Among the picture books written and illustrated by Ingpen are *The Idle Bear* in 1986, *The Dreamkeeper* in 1995 and *Who Is the World For*? in 2000. In the first, two worn teddy bears who have watched their owners grow up and leave them try to make sense of their place in the world. *The Dreamkeeper* was created by Ingpen for his granddaughter, Alice. Interweaving elements of reality and fantasy, he explains how the beings conjured up by human imaginations during dreams are kept from invading reality by a Dreamkeeper, who with the use of imaginative and intricately engineered traps and tools, returns all dream beings to their proper home in the Dreamtree.

Though Ingpen uses a variety of techniques and presentations, his style is distinct. He has a sure sense of perspective and composition and often emphasizes the effect of light and shadow. His paintings are authentic both in setting and historical detail, and the integrity of his vision reveals the emotional truth of the stories, while avoiding sentimentality. Through his paintings and illustrations Ingpen expresses his own deep feeling for an environment which is peculiarly Australian; especially its beaches, rivers and countryside. He paints the outward landscape of his country, but he also paints its hidden history, its soul and its people. His own "inner environment" gives an extra dimension to whatever subject he portrays. He brings to children's books a true and realistic appreciation of his own country, its past, its present and its potential. He also brings a perspective widened by travel and contact with other environments and cultures; an eye open to the differing qualities of light in many parts of the world. He sees beyond the face of a man, to his soul

The Voyage of The Poppy Kettle
冒險勇士七個半

THE POPPYKETTLE 'SILVERFISH'   INGPEN BOOK   P 49

The Ugly Duckling
醜小鴨

The Idle Bear
小熊的季節

If You Wish
願望

If You Wish 願望

杜桑凱利
DUŠAN KÁLLAY

捷克共和國　SLOVAKIA-REPUBLIC

1988

19世紀英國作家路易斯卡羅(Lewis Carroll)於1865年完成曠世名著《愛麗絲夢遊仙境》，150年來不斷有插畫家挑戰這個經典主題，塑造出風格、類型千變萬化的愛麗絲。杜桑凱利(1948-　)筆下的《愛麗絲夢遊仙境》，無疑是眾多插畫版本中最令人印象深刻的作品，黑髮小女孩和傳統的金髮愛麗絲大異其趣，仙境與鏡中奇遇的場景魔幻詭異而陰沈，色彩極盡瑰麗而超乎想像。

杜桑凱利的《愛麗絲夢遊仙境》1981年出版，1983年贏得「布拉迪斯國際插畫雙年展」(Biennial of Illustrations Bratislava，簡稱BIB)大獎，而後杜桑凱利於1988年獲頒國際安徒生大獎。

國際安徒生大獎史上，杜桑凱利是歷來四位「捷克斯洛伐克」插畫家的第二位得主，但自從「絲絨革命」促使捷克斯洛伐克聯邦和平解體，於1993年分別獨立為捷克共和國、斯洛伐克共和國，杜桑凱利便成為史上唯一的斯洛伐克得主。

杜桑凱利1948年生於斯洛伐克的首都布拉提斯瓦(Bratislava)，正是BIB的主辦地，這項國際插畫雙年展創立於1967年，形成僅次於波隆納的國際插畫盛會，由此可見插畫藝術在斯洛伐克的深耕厚植。

杜桑凱利的妻子史坦克洛娃(Kamila Stanclova)也是傑出的斯洛伐克插畫家，兩人結緣於就讀布拉提斯拉瓦藝術學院時，現今也同樣都在母校教書。這對插畫佳偶相知相戀相處數十年來，在藝術風格、技法相互影響，卻又各自保有獨特風格，因此受到巴黎、布拉格兩大出版社共同委託，於2001年啟動斯洛伐克史上最大規模的童書插畫計畫，由這對夫妻完成安徒生童話全數156部作品，分為三大卷，於2005年陸續出版。布拉提斯拉瓦市立美術館曾於2010年以「兩個神奇的世界」(Two Magical Worlds)為題，舉辦這對夫妻的雙人展，兩人的畫作也獲得不少歐美重要美術館收藏。

「對藝術家來說，能為美麗的文字畫插圖是種榮幸。我想感謝寫出文字的作家，讓我們有機會能認識他們的作品，尤其路易斯卡羅，他的作品總能不斷帶給我啟發。」杜桑凱利的國際安徒生大獎得獎感言，謙虛地將榮耀歸於作家，但對全球　的杜桑凱利迷而言，他的繪畫世界如絲縷密織的繁複線條、層次異常豐富的奇幻色彩、技藝絕佳的精湛手法，東歐民族獨特的神秘美感，更是吸引人閱讀繪本的魔法之鑰。

杜桑凱利迄今完成過兩百餘本童書插畫，也創作許多深富藝術性的蝕刻版畫，他的藝術才華擴及藏書票和郵票設計、動畫電影作品等。2002年，他以斯洛伐克郵政史為主題設計的郵票，還於奧地利維也納的國際郵展，贏得「世界最美的郵票」獎。

Born in Bratislava in 1948, Dušan Kállay is now professor at the Academy of Fine Arts in Bratislava where he studied graphic art, book illustration and painting . He has devoted himself to graphic art, book illustration, painting, design of ex libris and stamps, and animated films. He has illustrated several books for adults and numerous children's books, including titles by Walte Scott, Grimm and Carroll, for Slovak as well as for German, Austrian, Taiwanese and Japanese publishers.

Kállay is a graphic artist and painter both by profession and by nature. This fact gives direction to the style of his illustrations, in which graphically conceived drawing and pure painting techniques can be observed as the two fundamental forms. The typical touch of the graphic artist is represented by black-and-white illustrations done in pen-and-ink. These illustrations feature refined drawing with dynamic hatching and a sense of detail and symbol. Kállay prefers this type of expression particularly when illustrating books for adolescents.

The classical children's world of magical shapes and colours comes strikingly to the fore in his painted illustrations. Things hinted at or expressed by means of symbols in his drawings or graphic art are expressed more amply in his painted illustrations. The composition presenting the central motif in just the right relationship to the details achieves a pictorial entity that is enriched by his unique creation of a specific atmosphere.

Neither the drawn nor the painted illustrations are mere mechanical graphic transcriptions of the text. They are, above all, an expression of an interiorized text presented through the filter of his fantasy and imagination. The outcome of this process is an artistic form that conforms both to the text and to the artist's personality.

The illustrations to *Alice in Wonderland* show the full range of Kállay's ability to formulate his rich imagination in a refined and creative visual language. Kállay's Wonderland is lyrical, and his compositions bring a diversity of details into a harmonious whole. He enhances Carroll's fantasy and carefully places it on the threshold of children's imaginations. The simplicity and the fascinating secrecy of shapes, the colourful atmosphere, and the many elements of meaning within the framework of a single picture - all these appeal directly to young readers.

"Illustrating a beautiful text is a privilege for an artist. I would like to thank the authors of literary texts for giving us the possibility of getting to know their work, and especially Lewis Carroll, the author who is the closest to me. His work never ceases to inspire me." (From his Hans Christian Andersen Award acceptance speech).

H.C.Andersen Fairy Tales
安徒生童話

H.C.Andersen Fairy Tales
安徒生童話

H.C.Andersen Fairy Tales
安徒生童話

H.C.Andersen Fairy Tales
安徒生童話

莉絲白茨威格
LISBETH ZWERGER

奧地利　AUSTRIA

1990

「莉絲白茨威格在畫畫的時候，選擇站在人性的這邊，因此得以表現出童話故事和經典文學最深沉的意義。而且她很擅長留白的運用，用色細膩完美，還會出奇不意地混合幽默感和詩意，她筆下的人物也展現舞蹈般的動態，賦予她的作品非常現代的一面。初次看到的時候，感覺就像在看當代平面藝術家向傳統致敬。」

年僅36歲的女性插畫家，贏得1990國際年安徒生大獎評審團如此高度讚譽，莉絲白茨威格(1954-　)實至名歸，美麗、奇幻、怪誕、愉悅的感傷情懷，摻揉了動作、舞蹈、自然、幻想，全都加在一起後，成就了茨威格的藝術。

莉絲白茨威格1954年生於維也納，自小學業表現平平，曾經歷過一段找尋自我的過程，直到就讀維也納應用美術學院，接觸到捷克插畫大師傑利唐卡(Jiři Trnka)的作品，開啟茨威格想要創作插畫的念頭;當時與她交往的英國畫家約翰羅威(John Rowe)，介紹茨威格認識英國維多利亞時期插畫家亞瑟拉克漢(Arthur Rackham)等人作品，「我從中獲得很多啟發，開始懂得從故事中發掘其中況味，開始感受到自己似乎有這樣的使命。」茨威格說:「走上這條路並不是我所預期的，但卻是生命中自然而然發生的。」

茨威格尚未畢業就離開學校，嫁給約翰羅威，並投入插畫創作，年僅23歲，就於1977年出版第一本繪本《怪小孩》(The Strange Child)，此後，接連為各大名家的作品推出令人驚喜的圖像詮釋。

她的早期作品承襲英國維多利亞風格，《胡桃鉗》、《拇指姑娘》等作品皆帶有銅褐色調、線條粗獷、色塊分明等特點。1980年代的《伊索寓言》、《小紅帽》、《夜鶯》等作品，色調轉為明亮，並有細膩描繪，是為她的魔幻寫實時期。1990年代進入成熟期，茨威格信手拈來揮灑自如，創作出她最膾炙人口的代表作如《綠野仙蹤》、《愛麗絲夢遊仙境》。21世紀的茨威格正是創作高峰，將《小美人魚》、《布萊梅樂隊》等經典再創，並且再度取材《胡桃鉗》，以同一題材從不同人生階段展現生命的成長與淬煉。

溫暖、優雅、如歌的詩篇加上淺白又機智的幽默感，正是茨威格插畫的迷人魅力。「為童話繪製插畫，不是一種用大腦跟科學去詮釋的過程，而是轉化內在圖像和情感的工作。」茨威格總是細心閱讀文本，提煉原著最引人入勝的神髓，不斷試驗許多畫法和構圖，並且用色彩創造對比和點出主題，「身為插畫家，創作過程99%都在受苦，但在作品定稿、完成的一刻，就是最好的回報。」

Lisbeth Zwerger was born in 1954 in Vienna, where she studied at the College of Applied Art. Her aim was to become an illustrator, and it is in the classical fantasy and nonsense tales, fairy tales, legends, sagas and fables hat she found her sphere of work. She made her debut in 1977 when she chose to illustrate E.T.A. Hoffman's *The Strange Child*, and went on to enjoy If in surprising pictorial interpretations ranging from works by Dickens, Wilde, Nesbit, Grimm, Andersen, Carroll, Baum and Morgenstern to medieval legends such as *Till Eulenspiegel*. She finds her essential inspiration in English illustrators such as Rackham, Leech and Shepard.

She works in ink and watercolours - though in later years she has used gouache - and her illustrations have developed from the dark-toned and atmospheric characteristic of her first books, such as Hansel and Gretel, to an assured use of the whole palette, which makes the colours sparkle.

Her paintings are marked by a tender poetry, a lyricism and grace, combined with a robust and witty humour. She is faithful to the style and tone of the fairy tales, and the period in which they were created. Her illustrations for Andersen's fairy tales are delicately beautiful in their childlike simplicity, but at the same time she precisely captures the complexity within them.

She is the interpretive, not the explanatory illustrator. "To illustrate a fairy tale is not an intellectual, scientific interpretation, but a transposition of internal pictures and feelings." It is the story behind the text that she coaxes out, the mysterious, the unexpressed and, with the help of bold and unexpected pruning of images and unusual and supra forms, she achieves a completely individual, often grotesque effect. This appears, for instance, in *The Wizard of oz* and *Alice in Wonderland*, where she combines the text and pictures in a very refined graphical way that creates dynamism and movement. The comical pictures, with their mysterious hints, and her faithfulness to nature in portraying people and animals, create a tense contrast to the magical world of the stories.

"Lisbeth Zwerger takes sides when she paints. She takes the side of all that is human and, by doing so, she exposes the deepest meanings of fairy tales and classics. Furthermore, she does so with a fantastic use of space, with delicate perfection in her sense of colour, with an unexpected mixture of humour and poetry, with a dance-like movement in her characters that brings a very modern aspect to what, at first sight, seem a tribute to tradition in the work of a contemporary graphic artist." (From the Jury President's laudatio)

The beautiful, fantastic and grotesque, the cheerfulness and the melancholy, movement, dance, nature and fantasy all combine to make Zwerger's art. There is space in her illustrations, while, at the same time, she attends meticulously to detail. Her many representations of animals are completely true to nature, and yet full of imagination. "Without proper details, a picture cannot be lifelike - but without skilful use of free space, a picture cannot come alive."

Little Mermaid
小美人魚

Little Mermaid
小美人魚

Little Mermaid
小美人魚

Little Mermaid
小美人魚

Little Mermaid
小美人魚

柯薇塔
KVÉTA PACOVSKÁ

捷克 CZECH REPUBLIC

1992

「我創造的圖畫不是用來解釋文本的，我是建立一個讓藝術得以展現自我權力的有效空間。」柯薇塔(1928-)總是強調「我是藝術家，不是説書人」(I'm an artist, not a story teller)，她説：「我的圖畫，它們自己就是文本。」

這位滿頭白髮的捷克老太太，像個優雅的嬉皮，渾身上下都充滿活力、童心與自我主張，令她發熱發光的能量，正是發自內心的藝術態度。

1928年生於布拉格，柯薇塔來自藝術氣息濃厚的家庭，父親是歌劇歌手，母親是外語老師，從小就在書本、繪畫、音樂包圍下成長。然而，猶太人父親遭納粹殺害、柯薇塔被迫停學，陰霾的少女時代，唯有奶奶與故事書的陪伴注入溫暖，也種下柯薇塔成為畫家的種子。

二次大戰結束後，柯薇塔以優異成績獲得獎學金，進入布拉格應用藝術學院。她的老師埃米爾菲拉(Emil Filla)曾是20世紀初捷克最早的立體派團體「奧薩馬」(Osma，意指「八人組」)成員，與作家卡夫卡也經常往來，埃米爾菲拉更成為捷克前衛藝術的重要領航員。

深受現代藝術薰陶的柯薇塔，醉心於康定斯基、克利、米羅、畢卡索等藝術 家作品，發展出構圖簡潔、形色明快的視覺藝術風格，遊走於藝術創作與平面設計領域，自1961年以來舉辦過數十次展覽。直到成為母親之後，回憶起兒時從繪本得到的感動，柯薇塔才開始嘗試為孩子繪製童書。

1984年出版第一本童書以來，柯薇塔創作近60本作品，涵蓋題材極廣。她的書有種動感，流露出她説故事時的喜悅，她也經常把圖像從傳遞訊息的媒介，變成小朋友可以親自動手實驗、互動的物品，許多本書都展現了她大玩形狀、顏色、空間、線條的功力。1992年出版號稱世界上最美的書《字母書》(Alphabet)，翻折26個字母變成立體，每個字母都有各自的性格與故事，翻開每一頁都是驚喜。

1992年，國際安徒生大獎將插畫桂冠頒予64歲的柯薇塔，她永不停滯的創作之心，卻像1993年才誕生的捷克共和國，孩子般一路狂奔。

1993年，她以《太陽是黃色的》(The Sun is Yellow)、《午夜探險》(Midnight Play)兩本書同時入圍波隆納國際兒童書展的最佳選書獎；此後《賣火柴的小女孩》、《灰姑娘 》、《小小花國國王》的顏色、形狀趣味，更是處理得洗練極致。

去年，柯薇塔以87歲高齡來台舉辦個展，成熟的童心、超越歲月的自信丰采，以凡人難及的境界，向喜愛她的讀者示範了真正的藝術家風範。

Born in 1928 in Prague, Kvéta Pacovská graduated from the PragueSchool of Applied Arts, where she studied under Professor Emil Filla, a representative of Czech modernism, who introduced his students to the European avant-garde.

Kvéta Pacovská has created images which merge the artistic tradition of children's book illustrators with perceptible influences from classical modern artists, such as Kandinsky, Schwitters, Klee, Miro and Picasso. Her creative work includes painting, graphic and applied art and book illustration. She operates in the domain between the free graphic arts and illustration. She draws, paints, creates collages and all conceivable things with paper, which in her hands becomes a playground for exciting experiments linking image and text.

Pacovská herself has created several books for small children. Her books have a dynamic quality and reveal her joy in telling stories involving the fabulous creations of her imagination. Poetic atmosphere and imagination turn her books into rare works of art.

Eins, finf viele (One, Five, Many) in 1990 and *Grun, rot, alle (Green, Red, All)* in 1992 are examples of development of the medium of the picture into an object which children can interact with for their own experiments. In these books Pacovskáexhibits her talent for playing with forms, colours spaces and lines.

Some motifs turn up again and again in this humorous picture world and - often as a collage - play a kind of symbolic role: windows, eyes, shoes beaks, pencils, cats, cherries, clowns and sheets of music.

Kvéta Pacovská's huge output - close to sixty books - covers a wide range, including illustrations to Andersen, Grimm and Michael Ende. She has also held numerous one-woman shows, and regularly takes part in international art and illustration exhibitions around the world.

"A drawing is such as it is. It should not and cannot pretend. It expresses our feelings and our thoughts", she says. "I'm striving for maximum contrast. Red and green. Green is vivid and red is cheerful! Additionally, there is black, holding all colours in it, and white as the "pure" colour. The placing of colours one over the other. It depends on the relation, proportion, rhythm, size, amount, and how we place colours together. It is like music. Each individual tone is beautiful by itself and in certain groupings we create dimensions, harmony, disharmony. Symphonies, operas. And books for children."

The Little Flower King
小花國王

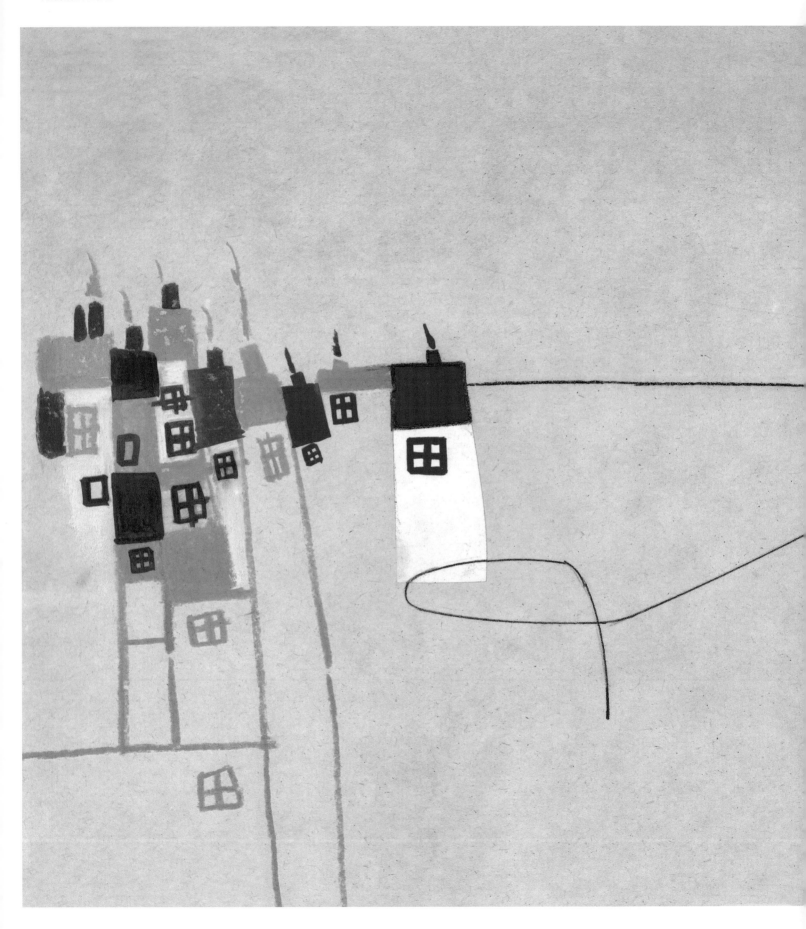

The Little Flower King
小花國王

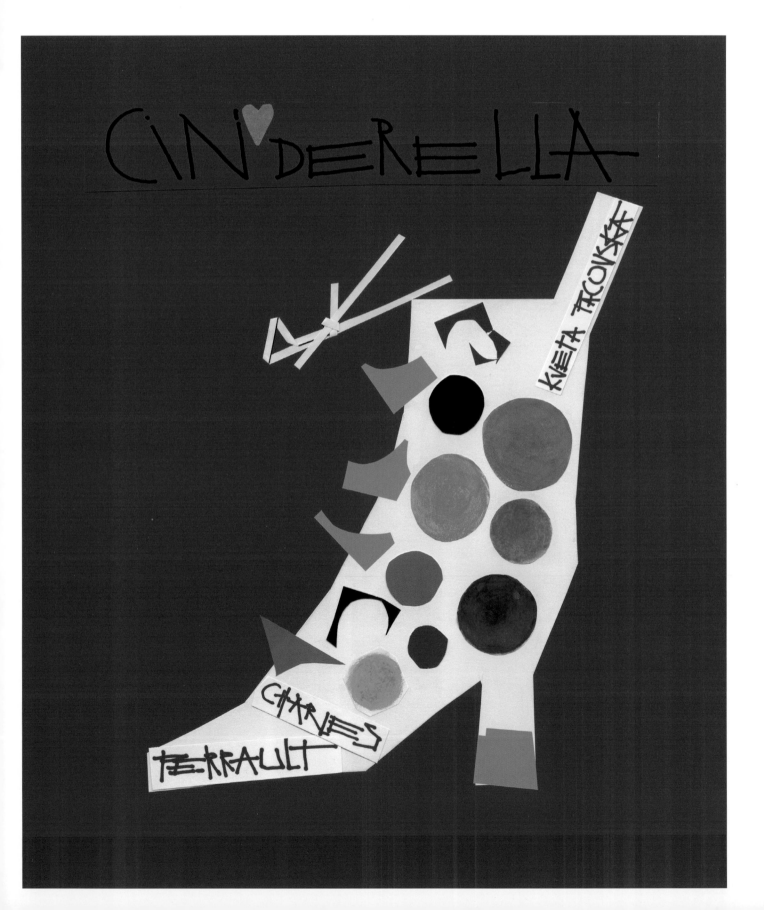

Cinerella
灰姑娘

My Bedtime Monster
我的床邊怪獸

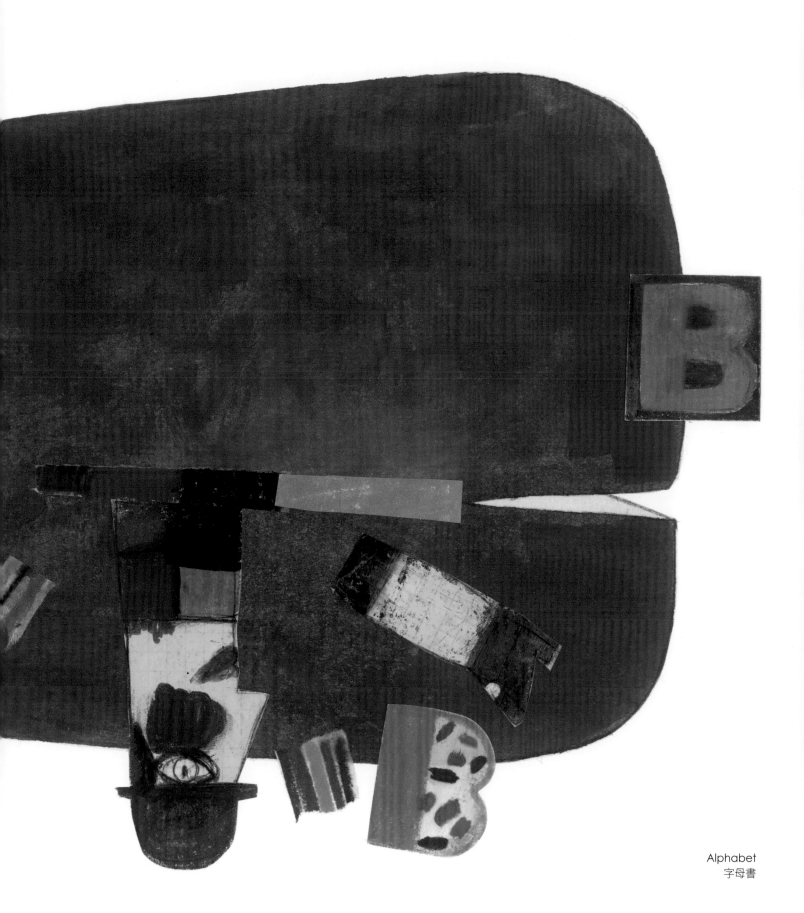

Alphabet
字母書

約克米勒
JÖRG MÜLLER

瑞士   SWITZERLAND

1994

「約克米勒的作品遠比單純的寫實畫作更豐富動人。」瑞士童書評論家塞特琳（Josiane Cetlin）曾如此評述：「在他的作品中的每一樣東西都表現得栩栩如生，而讀者們也可以感受到他畫作中層次豐富的想像空間。」

深入品賞約克米勒(1942-)作品，會發現超凡的想像力，來自藝術家深思熟慮的良知投射，正是這份蘊含的深意，為約克米勒贏來1994年國際安徒生大獎。

約克米勒1942年生於瑞士洛桑，自蘇黎世和比爾(Biel)的應用藝術學校畢業之後，曾在巴黎從事平面藝術創作。

1973年，米勒推出繪本處女作《挖土機年年作響－鄉村變了》(The Changing Countryside)，一出版就獲得極高評價；1976年，他以相同手法創作姐妹作《城市的改變》，描繪欠缺考慮的都市開發帶來的破壞。這兩本書在當時造成相當大的震撼，不僅揭示人們內心潛心的恐懼，同時啟迪了無數兒童青少年的思維。

米勒的作品常被視為「綠繪本」代表，環境問題向來是米勒關注的焦點，但他並不宣揚「回歸大自然」的說教手法，而是呈現一個真實的世界，讓讀者打開他們的眼睛，去觀察、發現並且思索自己身處的生活環境。

《挖土機年年作響－鄉村變了》全書只有七幅圖畫，呈現同一地點、每隔三年左右的景觀變化，一處風光明媚的鄉村小屋，從炊煙繚繞的家園，變成廢棄的房舍，而後被拆除成為大馬路旁的商店……，沒有任何文字，即凸顯出環境開發付出的代價。

環境問題延伸到自身存在價值的省思，賦予米勒作品更深刻的哲學性。米勒和作家約克史坦納(Jorg Steiner)自1976年開始，合作多本寓意深遠的繪本，《森林大熊》(The bear who wanted to stay a bear)描繪一覺醒來已身在人類世界的熊，傳達文明入侵的無奈;1977年《再見了! 小兔子》(Die Kanincheninse)講述兩隻兔子逃離安逸但無聊的「兔子工廠」，投入大自然的懷抱，大灰兔卻已經過不慣生命飽受威脅的日子，寧可揮別小褐兔，回到禁錮但「無憂無慮」的生活。

1994年獲得國際安徒生大獎肯定之後，約克米勒仍然創作不懈、迭有佳作。1996年的無字繪本《發現小錫兵》，將安徒生童話《小錫兵》以現代精神重新詮釋，探討垃圾/ 再生議題，遭遺棄的小錫兵竟然在非洲父子的巧手改裝下，成為巴黎的博物館收藏。

總是不斷挑戰創作形式的米勒，在2001年《書中之書中之書….》(Das Buch im Buch im Buch)大玩書本結構，巧手描繪讓小主角一層一層深入書中的折射空間。無限到底有沒有盡頭呢？約克米勒正是以這樣的發掘精神，探索著繪本的極限與無盡可能。

Jörg Müller was born in 1942 in Lausanne. He graduated from the School of Applied Arts in Zurich and Biel, then worked as a graphic artist in Paris for several years.

His first picture book *Alle Jahre wieder saust der Presslutthammer nieder. Die Veranderung der Landschaft (The Changing Countryside)* in 1973 was a portfolio of paintings depicting the gradual urbanization of an idyllic rural area. It immediately became an enormous international success, which encouraged Müller to create a sequel about the destruction of a cityscape through untrammelled and thoughtless urbanization.

Müller's first collaboration with the writer Jorg Steiner, in 1976, was a book version of a film project Müller had done for German television, called *Der Bar, der ein Bar bleiben wollte (The bear who wanted to stay a bear)*. It formed the basis of a partnership which has continued for many years and t resulted in a long series of works, several of which have achieved classic status, as for instance *Die Kanincheninsel* (1977) about the risk of achieving freedom despite the fear of the unknown. Two rabbits flee from a factory where they live a boring but secure life. Freedom is beautiful but dangerous and one of them finally returns to the factory. Müller is a master at visualising the landscape. He combines dream and reality in a splendid composition and is simultaneously poetic and realistic.

After a number of other books together, Müller and Steiner returned to the animal fable. For *The Animals' Rebellion or The New City Musicians*, in 1989, Müller developed a cinematographic style of surprising perspectives to accompany his attention to detail and his use of black and fluorescent colours. Four animals, well-known as trademarks in advertising, want to escape from their commercial exploitation but in the end part company. Only one of them, the Panda bear, tries to seek freedom outside, where the winds blow but also loneliness awaits. The story is developed in sequences like a television programme and each page is framed like a TV screen. Are we reading a book or watching television?

Müller's wordless interpretation of Andersen's well-known tale of *The Steadfast Tin Soldier* transports the story into a modern world, where ecological issues and the North-South problem are especially prominent. He achieves stunning effects on large, meticulously designed double spreads, full of details and quotations from his other works.

In *Das Buch im Buch im Buch* Müller plays with the structure of books and lets his small principal character delve deeper and deeper into the many layers of the book. Anything can happen in this "mirrored" reality.

Müller seems to prefer large format books, where his art unfolds powerfully in portfolio, oblong or square. The double spreads offer him space, allowing him to divide pages into further spaces. His range of colours is wide, but each volume has its own tonality. Whatever the format, Jörg Müller's book deal with essential issues that concern us all : loss of instinct and identity, the complexity of the question of liberty, the meaning of life and the values one gives it.

Alarm in carpet Reich
地毯王國的警報

再見，小兔子！

Die Kanincheninsel
再見，小兔子！

Die Kanincheninsel
再見，小兔子！

El soldadito de plomo
發現小錫兵

El soldadito de plomo
發現小錫兵

克勞斯恩西卡特
KLAUS ENSIKAT

德國　GERMANY

1996

半生歲月都在鐵幕度過，1996年國際安徒生大獎得主克勞斯恩西卡特(1937-　　)，看過柏林圍牆築起又崩塌，經歷過東西陣營的長期冷戰對峙，走過波濤洶湧的時代巨變，他的插畫以一種日耳曼式的冷靜，構築嚴謹縝密的線條世界，並在略帶誇張的異化手法下，展現慧黠之光的幽默。

恩西卡特1937年生於東柏林，在二次世界大戰的烽火中度過童年，而後1949年東西德分裂，直到1990年兩德統一，長達41年都生活在蘇聯占領的前東德。

他自1951年便接受商業畫師的訓練，繼而於1954年進入東柏林應用美術學院攻讀商業藝術。恩西卡特作品的緻密線條，帶有濃厚的19世紀德國浪漫主義蝕刻版畫韻致，便得力於這所學校特別重視手繪字、排版和印刷，所奠定的紮實基礎。

恩西卡特擅用細鉛筆和鵝毛筆勾勒線條，再以半透明或不透明水彩填色，一絲不苟呈現所有物體、服裝、臉部表情、甚至是暗示動作的微小細節。他偏愛將手繪字、縮寫字母、藤蔓圖案等裝飾元素注入畫作，也發展出融合書寫藝術和書籍插畫技巧的獨特風格。

1960年，克勞斯恩西卡特的繪畫作品首見於文化周報《Sonnetag》，而後在諷刺雜誌《Eulenspiegel》刊出。特別的是，他的弟弟彼得恩西卡特(Peter Ensikat，1941-2013)日後成為著名的東德卡巴萊(Cabaret)劇作家，而這種在歐洲小酒館中載歌載舞又帶有話劇形式的娛樂表演，和諷刺畫(Caricature)經常出現誇張、怪誕的形象淵源頗深。

恩西卡特一度於1961年至1965年間任教於母校，而後自1965年以自由藝術家的身份，繪製書籍插畫、從事平面設計和字型設計的工作。兩德統一之後，他於1995年至2002年擔任漢堡造型藝術高等專科學院教授，現居柏林。

創作至少上百本書籍插畫，包括德國文豪歌德名著《浮士德》、席勒的經典歌劇《威廉泰爾》等古典傑作。他取材自英國作家托爾金奇幻小說《哈比人的冒險》於1971年創作的插畫，翌年為他贏得波隆納最佳選書獎；而他的近年插畫作品如《聖經的故事》、《兒童大學》系列、《小馬兒的聖誕節》等，都一如恩希卡特認為，插畫必須超越原文、加強對故事的詮釋，甚至找到文字無法觸及的管道，在小朋友翻動書頁的時候，喚醒他們的想像力，並以適度的張力來誘使小朋友更進一步發問與思考。

Born in Berlin in 1937, Klaus Ensikat began his career in 1951 as an apprentice commercial designer, then in 1954 started to study commercial arts at the East Berlin University of Applied Art, where the emphasis was on lettering, typesetting and printing. He thus received a thorough grounding in the draughtsmanship which was later to stand him in good stead as an illustrator of children's books. After finishing his studies, he worked for two years as a designer in an advertising firm. In 1960 his drawings first appeared in *Sonntag*, a cultural weekly, then in the satirical magazine *Eulenspiegel*. Soon he was designing book jackets for the East Berlin publisher Aufbau Verlag. In 1961-65 he taught at the East Berlin University of Applied Arts. By 1965 he started working on his own, and since then has supported himself as a freelance artist, doing graphic design and typography but most of all book illustrations. Since 1995 he has been teaching book illustration at the University of Applied Arts in Hamburg.

An illustration, in Ensikat's view, has to go beyond the actual text in facilitating interpretation of the story and helping to make the characters come alive for the readers. Sometimes the illustrator can find channels unexplored by the text to awaken children's imaginations as they turn the pages of the book. Ensikat is strongly opposed to drawings which display a perfect and artificially imposed harmony. He believes that each picture must contain a certain amount of tension or friction in order to entice children into investigating what really matters and challenge them to ask questions. He considers himself as a partner to his authors, but one whose illustrations take the reader one step further than the text.

Ensikat has mastered every form of illustration, but the unique style he has developed is a synthesis of the techniques of calligraphy and book illustration. He draws fully detailed pictures with fine pencil and quill pen lines, filling them with translucent or opaque watercolours. Every minute detail of an object, clothing, facial expression, even the hint of movement is rendered with meticulous and painstaking care through his fine hatchings. Judging from his lettering and his use of decorative elements such as initials and vignettes, he has a strong bent toward old traditions of book illustration. He has put this substantial array of skills to work in illustrating children's books, incorporating traditional techniques into his individual artistic vision.

Klaus Ensikat has no idea how many books he has illustrated for children, but it is certain that his wildly fantastical creatures in period costumes, from mice and cats to peacocks and wolves, and his varied human characters, from Victorian gentlemen and villagers to adventurous little girls and princesses, appear in more than a hundred books.

The Peacock's Wedding
孔雀的婚禮

The Peacock's Wedding
孔雀的婚禮

Eine Woche lang kam der Fuchs nicht aus seiner Höhle heraus.
Er aß und trank den lieben langen Tag und gab keinem was ab.
Nur den Hasen lud er zu einem Gläschen Rotwein ein.
Es wird bestimmt die Marke „Löwenblut" gewesen sein.

„Und jetzt *Wein her!*" keckerte der Fuchs. Da wankte der Hase mit dem Rotwein in den Saal. Er zitterte vor lauter Angst in einem fort und goss beim

The Peacock's Wedding
孔雀的婚禮

Dann eine Katze mit einem samtschwarzen Fell.

Das A steht vorn im Alphabet
字母童話

Ach, J!

J j

Das A steht vorn im Alphabet
字母童話

湯米溫格爾
TOMI UNGERER

法國　FRANCE

1998

1998年國際安徒生大獎評審團，盛讚湯米溫格爾(1931-)是「兒童繪本創作世界的大巨人」，實際上，湯米溫格爾作風大膽、創新、叛逆又獨特，非凡人所能消受。他從被封殺的「童書界壞小子」，峰迴路轉贏得舉世推崇，已寫下逆轉勝的當代傳奇。

「每次回顧我的人生，我都感到害怕，恐懼人生。」湯米溫格爾說：「這很好，因為一旦有了恐懼，就要想辦法找到存活的勇氣。」

湯米溫格爾1931年生於法國亞爾薩斯省的史特拉斯堡，納粹占領的陰影籠罩著童年。1956年，25歲的溫格爾帶著對自由的嚮往飛往美國。1957年出版第一本童書《梅隆斯去飛翔》(The Mellops Go Flying)。

「他曾是美國最有名的童書作家，後來便銷聲匿跡……。」2012年紀錄片《童心未泯湯米溫格爾》(Far Out Isn't Far Enough: The Tomi Ungerer Story)，開場白便是這段耐人尋味的話。

1960年代，湯米溫格爾非常活躍，是個十分多產、且創作方向多元的藝術家。就連美國插畫大師莫里斯桑達克也讚歎「天份、天份、渾然天成」。桑達克說：「湯米是非常瘋狂的。」而這份瘋狂，成為桑達克創作《野獸國》的能量之一。溫格爾的童書創作，總不忌諱讓孩子看到生活的黑暗面：　1961《三個強盜》(The Three Robbers)證明善惡不是二分法; 1966《月亮先生》(Moon Man)反映對外來者的排擠; 1999年《奧圖》(Otto: Biography of a Teddy Bear)透過一隻德國來的老泰迪熊，鋪陳帶有自傳色彩的故事，講述戰爭的生離死別。他的創造力百無禁忌，畫政治漫畫反對越戰、種族隔離主義，曾為一家夜店設計情色風格的海報，甚至於1969年出版成人書《Fornicon》，造成極大爭議。「畫A書的人怎麼可以畫童書呢？」那年的美國圖書年會(ALA)上，溫格爾面對 質疑不改本色，做出兒童不宜的反駁，導致他的童書在全美圖書館被禁長達二十多年。溫格爾憤而離開美國，輾轉多處之後，隱居愛爾蘭鄉間生活。雖然在美國「銷聲匿跡」，他的藝術成就還是廣受肯定，法國、德國先後頒贈溫格爾勳章，1998年安徒生大獎、2003歐洲童書大使、2007湯米溫格爾美術館在他的家鄉成立，都是對這位藝術家的致敬。

時間是最好的裁判，當年溫格爾的無畏衝撞，成了今時的英雄，2012年大獲好評的溫格爾記錄片是由美國拍攝完成，溫格爾2012年童書《霧島》(Fog Island)也於翌年獲紐約時報的年度最佳十本童書，重新用插畫征服美國。數十年過去了，老湯米仍是辛辣、百無禁忌的溫格爾，他說：「我對白紙充滿敬意，敬完之後就拿我的畫或寫作強暴它。」頑皮一笑，他正經說：「因為只有當你的生命被搶奪，新的人生才會開始，這張紙便有了新人生。當這張紙被印成書，它有了第二個新生命。」而後，「當這本書被閱讀的時候，它就有第三生命了!」

Tomi Ungerer was born in Strasburg, Alsace, in 1931 and was already beginning to draw at the age of ten, against the background of the German occupation of the region. The drawings, which capture the occupying power with extraordinary maturity, being both satirical and serious, have been recorded in the autobiographical *À la guerre comme à la guerre (Tom, A Childhood Under the Nazis)*.

Ungerer has been called the 'enfant terrible' of children books because of his black human and provoking refusal to compromise. The morbidly grotesque is characteristic of his work, which includes picture books and illustrator books for children and adults, political satire, cartoons and erotic sketches, caricatures and posters as well as other media. The close proximity of the war, he says, gave him a sense of the macabre.

He chooses his artistic expression with care. His political satire is caustic in a refined and sophisticated manner, while as illustrator of *Das grosse Liederbuch (The Great Songbook)*, for instance, he can create perfect thumbnail impression of great intensity and involvement with just a few lines and pencil stroke.

His picture books are simple, wry and grotesque; you can go exploring in his pictures, bursting with colour, with surprising details, silhouette effects, soft yet precise outlines, and changing, plastic forms. He follows the traditions of the fairy tale, fable and classical children's book, by using animals and strange creatures to represent human frailty and folly: the lonely *Moon Man*; the absurd tale of the weird creature that eats M. Racine's wonderful pears; the young tearaway *Piper Paw in No Kiss for Mother*, where the satirises mother's complaints and children's need for freedom; and the three robber who discover that they have more fun in doing good than bad.

After a twenty-year break Tomi Ungerer returned to picture books in 1997. This long break was partly the result of being blacklisted in the United States, where it was difficult to accept him as a children's book illustrator, when, at the same time, he was producing political satire and erotica for adults.

1999 saw the publication of the picture book *Otto: Biography of a Teddy Bear*, a penetrating accounting of an old teddy's life from Germany in the 1930s-at the time the Jewish persecution and beginning of World Wall II-to the brash and chaotic United States of today. This book is a long distance from the spectacular effects that characterized Ungerer's earlier books. Text and pictures complement each other, and without overtly seeking for effect, the story ranges in its quite unique atmosphere from the quietly shocking to warm attachment and hope. Seldom has Ungerer's message of peace and tolerance emerged as clearly as in his book.

Ungerer is an artist of the unexpected: the surprise factor is essential to his books, and as an artist he has startled by constantly renewing himself, and by dealing with taboos and political correctness.

辛爺爺的怪獸

The Beast of Monsieur Racine
辛爺爺的怪獸

安東尼布朗
ANTHONY BROWNE

英國　UNITED　KINGDOM

2000

布朗1946年出生於雪菲爾。他在里茲(Leeds)修過一門平面設計課，其後又當了多年的賀卡設計師和醫學素描家才進入童書的世界。「我學到怎麼用圖畫説一個看起來很逼真，但實際上不是真的的故事(手術的故事)。」

他畫出世上最酷的猩猩一「…猩猩是…很大、孔武有力、長相兇猛，但是很溫柔、細膩、敏感的動物。」猩猩強壯、有力(可以掌控情況和自身的存在)的形象和溫暖、溫和、敏感的內在所形成的對比，對小朋友的自尊和情緒發展很重要。他在許多繪本作品中都用猩猩這個主題來描繪小朋友所熟悉的衝突。譬如說在威利系列裡，威利這隻拿不定主意又膽小的猩猩，就是透過想像力學會接受自己，找到跨越界線的勇氣，放手去做他不相信自己能做到的事。或是在《Gorilla》中，小女孩的玩具猩猩活生生出現在她夢中，給了她她渴望從父親身上得到的友誼和關愛。

他的作品所傳遞的訊息很嚴肅，他探討人際關係的意義，為彼此騰出時間的價值，玩樂和友情所帶來的喜悅。他的書讓我們看到這些基本價值被忽略時，孩子會多麼寂寞無助。但他出書不是為了爭論這些問題，相反地，他的訊息藉由想像力的力量清楚傳達出來。

布朗的作品常被歸類為超現實主義，其中馬格利特(Magritte)更是他一再在書中「引用」的對象，《夢想家威利》即是一例。他展現出日常物品和活動不同的面相，顛覆現實，賦予日常事物新的意義。他在《Changes》和《愛麗絲夢遊仙境》中都使用了這種手法，風趣的插畫成功捕捉後者故事中荒謬又美好的夢境。

他書中的文字通常很短很簡單，色彩明亮的插畫本身就已經自成一個世界。他為自己神奇的圖畫世界下了魔咒，裡面沒有一個東西是他表面上看起來的樣子。他筆下的世界充滿了令人不安的預兆、令人費解的秘密和微妙的細節。在《The Tunnel》一書中，一對兄妹穿越狹窄的隧道後，來到一處神秘的森林，裡面盡是奇怪又恐怖的動物，原本意見不合的兩人在這裡漸漸團結起來…。這個刺激又充滿寓意的故事帶給讀者許多不同層面的啟示。《Voices in the Park》很有意思，講的是兩家人到公園散步的故事。在四個短篇章裡面，四位主角(又是擬人化的猩猩)針對相同的事件，講出不同版本的故事，他特地選了四種不同的字體來表現不同的聲音。

布朗是位「有著不凡才情、出色技巧和無人能及的想像力的藝術家。他將繪本插畫帶到新境界。他細膩又發人深省的作品常被評為『超現實』；這些書總會讓大人小孩忍不住一看再看。」(2000年國際安徒生插畫大獎評審)

Born in Sheffield in 1946, Browne's route to children's books was via a graphic design course in Leeds, followed by some years making a living as a designer of greeting cards and as a medical artist. "I learned a lot about the telling of a story (the story of an operation) in images that seem to be realistic, but in fact aren't".

He paints the most fantastic gorillas"...gorillas are... huge, powerful, fierce-looking creatures, who are actually gentle, delicate, sensitive animals." It is just this contrast between the strong and the powerful — being able to hold one's own and control one's own existence — and the warm, gentle and sensitive, which is of vital importance to a child's self-esteem and emotional life. He uses the gorilla motif in many of his picture books to depict conflicts familiar to every child. For instance, he does this in the Willy books, about an uncertain and frightened wimp of a gorilla — who with the help of imagination learns to accept himself for what he is, finding the courage to cross boundaries and daring to do what he had not believed he could do; or in *Gorilla*, where a girl's toy gorilla becomes alive in her dreams and gives her the friendship and interest that she wants from her father.

The message of his book is serious; they deal with the meaning of human relationships, the value of having time for each other, the joy of play and friendships. They show how lonely and powerless children are when these basic values are neglected. But his books are not created in order to debate problems — on the contrary, his message comes across through the power of imagination.

Browne's work is allied to the surrealists, especially to Magritte, whom he 'quotes' time after time in his books (in *Willy the Dreamer*, among others). He shows different aspects of everyday things and events and turns reality upside down, enabling it to assume new meanings. He does this in *Changes*, and in his witty illustrations for *Alice in Wonderland*, capturing the story's wonderfully absurd dream world.

The texts of his book are generally short and simple, the bright colours of the illustrations a world in themselves. He casts a spell with his magical pictorial universe, where nothing is what it seems to be. A world filled with disquieting omens, puzzling secrets and subtle details. In *The Tunnel* a journey through a narrow tunnel brings two quarrelling siblings together in a mysterious landscape with peculiar and frightening beings — an exciting and symbolic story that unfolds at many levels. *Voices in the Park* is a fascinating story of two families walking in the park. In the four brief chapters the four main characters — once again anthropomorphic gorilla — tell their different versions of the same events, visualised through the choice of typesetting.

Browne is "an artist of unusual talent, exceptional technical skill and unrivalled imagination who has taken picture book illustration into new dimension. 'Surreal' is a word often applied to his subtle, challenging books which send children and adults back to them again and again." (The Hans Christian Andersen Award Jury 2000)

Willy the Wimp
膽小鬼威利

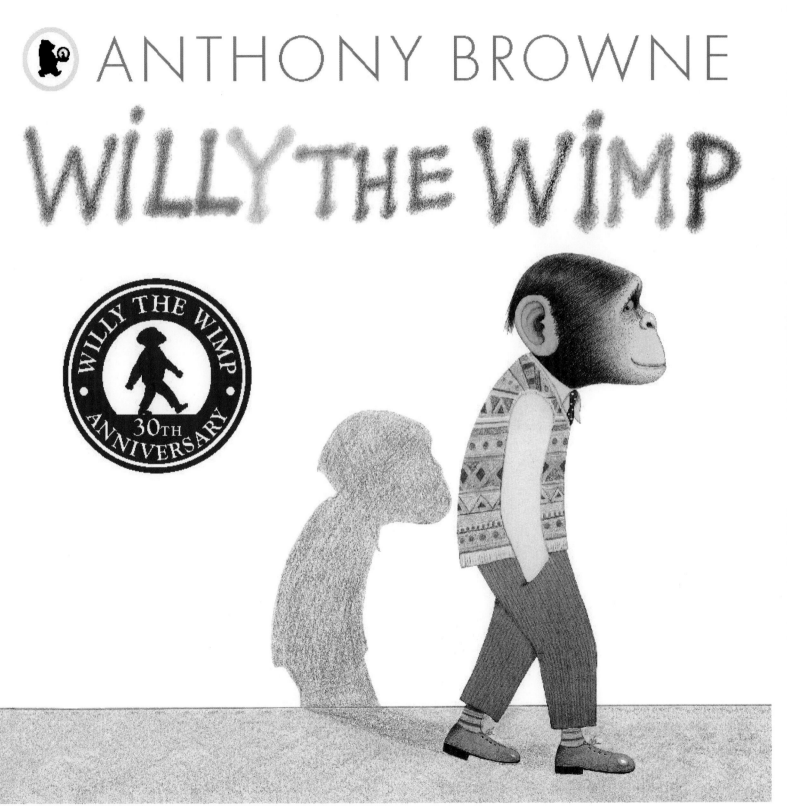

Copyright © 1984 Anthony Browne
From WILLY THE WIMP by Anthony Browne
Reproduced by permission of Walker
Books Ltd, London SE11 5HJ

Willy the Dreamer
夢想家威利

Copyright © 1997 Anthony Browne
From WILLY THE DREAMER by Anthony Browne
Reproduced by permission of Walker
Books Ltd, London SE11 5HJ

Willy the Dreamer
夢想家威利

Copyright © 1997 Anthony Browne
From WILLY THE DREAMER by Anthony Browne
Reproduced by permission of Walker
Books Ltd, London SE11 5HJ

Gorilla
大猩猩

Copyright © 1983 Anthony Browne
From GORILLA by Anthony Browne
Reproduced by permission of Walker
Books Ltd, London SE11 5HJ

Little Beauty
大猩猩與小星星

Copyright © 2008 Brun Limited
From LITTLE BEAUTY by Anthony Browne
Reproduced by permission of Walker
Books Ltd, London SE11 5HJ

昆丁布雷克
QUENTIN BLAKE

英國　UNITED　KINGDOM

2002

昆丁布雷克1932年生於英國肯特郡錫德卡普(Sidcup)，自有記憶以來一直都在作畫。早在16歲時，作品已首次刊登於《Punch》雜誌。他於劍橋大學道寧學院修讀英國文學後，在倫敦大學取得教育碩士學位，於1958至1959年間就讀切爾西藝術學校(Chelsea School of Art)，而後為《Punch》雜誌及《The Spectator》擔任插畫家及封面畫家。他在1978到1996年間擔任皇家藝術學院插畫系主任，自1988年起為該系資深研究員及訪問教授。

布雷克在1968年出版了第一本童書《Patrick》，此後他不但編繪自己的繪本，還為其他作家畫了兩百多本童書，合作對象包括路易斯卡羅、吉卜林、儒勒凡爾納、希薇亞普拉斯、瓊艾肯、羅爾德達爾、羅素霍班、邁克爾羅森、尤曼。他的畫作好笑、樸實、狂野，一點也不正經。畫中的人物一舉一動都散發出會傳染的喜悅。他的作品風格是典型的英國卡通畫作，不難看出《Punch》的痕跡。他用墨水所創作出來的素描輕盈優雅、簡潔有力。他的作品大多不是被搬上舞台演出，就是很適合大聲朗讀給幾個小朋友或一群人聽。

昆丁布雷克已經教出好幾代英國童書插畫家。以下是他給年輕插畫家的建議：「你必須時時渴望作畫，因為那是你能變厲害的不二法門。你可以研究一堆技巧，但是動手畫才是關鍵。除此之外，我不想給其他建議，因為當一個插畫家或童書作家主要的重點在於你是很多元素加在一起的混種…我比較在乎人一他們的表情和動作。如果你天生就想畫畫，用圖像說故事，你可以用很多不同的方式去產生貢獻。你可以看其他畫家的作品，但不要太受影響。繼續畫，繼續工作，你才能找到自己喜歡的東西，找到你能做的貢獻。這件事是沒有規則可循的。每個人都得靠自己去發現。」

「昆丁布雷克充滿活力和創意，這位偉大的藝術家無疑為兒童文學和兒童的世界作出了長遠的貢獻。他過去得過的各個獎項，並獲選為英國首位兒童文學桂冠作家(Children's Laureate)就是最好的證明。他的原創性和幽默感，還有對線條、色彩和動作的掌握，使他成為受人愛戴、影響國際的重量級插畫家。」（2002年國際安徒生插畫大獎評審）。

Quentin Blake was born in 1932 in Sidcup, Kent, England. He has drawn ever since he can remember. His first published drawing appeared in *Punch* magazine when he was only sixteen. After studies in English literature at Downing College, Cambridge, he took a postgraduate certificate in Education at London University, attended the Chelsea School of Art 1958-1959, and worked thereafter as illustrator and cover artist for *Punch* and *The Spectator*. He was Head of illustration Department of the Royal College of Art during 1978-96 and from 1988 its Senior Fellow and Visiting Professor.

In 1968, Blake published his first book for children, *Patrick*, and since then he has written and illustrated his own pictured books as well as illustrated over two hundred titled by other authors such as Lewis Carroll, Rudyard Kipling, Jules Verne, Sylvia Plath, Joan Aiken, Roald Dahl, Russell Hoban, Michael Rosen and John Yeoman, His drawing are funny, down-to-earth, wild and totally free from earnestness. In all of them there is a contagious joyfulness expressed in the movement and body language of the characters. His style is typical of the British cartoon; traces of *Punch* are obviously. Apparently simple, the drawings in Indian ink have the vitality, elegance and lightness of the sketch. Many of his books lend themselves to being performed and are excellent to read aloud and share with individual children or with a group.

Quentin Blake has taught several generations of English illustrators for children. This is the advice he offer to young artists: "You must want to draw all the time, because that is the only way you can get good at it. You can study a certain amount of technique, but doing it is the key element. Beyond that, I am disinclined to prescribe anything because one of the main aspects of being an illustrators or a children's author is what you are hybrid, a mixture of many elements...I tend to be concerned with people¬ – the face they make and the way they move. If you have the instinct to want to draw and to tell stories in pictures, there are many different things one might contribute. Look at the other artists' work but don't be too influenced by them. Go on drawing, go on doing the job, and you will find what you really like, and what you have contribute. In these sense, there are no rules. Everybody's got to find out for himself. "

"Vivacious and creative, Quentin Blake is a great artist who has clearly made a lasting contribution both to children's literature and to the world of children. This is evident from his many previous awards and his election as the United Kingdom's first Children Laureate. His originality and sense of humour, together with his skill with line, colours and movement have made him a beloved illustrator with wide international impact." (The Hans Christian Anderson Jury 2002)

Old Doreen
老多琳

Doreen

Chocolatier with a Cauldron
巧克力商和他的神奇魔法鍋

The Mayor - (Mr Baddlejoy)

The Mayor - (Mr. Baddlejoy)
市長－巴德喬伊先生

馬克思維特惠思
MAX VELTHUIJS

荷蘭　NETHERLANDS

2004

小青蛙「弗洛格」(Frog) 與他的朋友，是荷蘭繪本大師馬克思維特惠思 (1923-2005) 畢生創作中，最膾炙人口的角色，色彩明快、樸拙無華的視覺風格，勾勒出溫暖、睿智而幽默的世界，傳達大自然、動物、人類和諧共存之愛。

維特惠思1923年生於海牙，曾於荷蘭東部城市安恆 (Arnhem) 的視覺藝術學院 (Academie voor Beeldende Kunsten) 修讀繪畫與平面設計，1944年因戰火而輟學習。二次世界大戰結束之後，維特惠思回到海牙，製作政治版畫，並接受委託印製海報、郵票、書籍封面、動畫影片、廣告等，經由這段實務歷練，維特惠思發現，他最想專心發展的志業，是繪製、設計書籍。

1960年代，維特惠思投注他的創作才華成為插畫家。1962年，他為荷蘭一家出版社編纂的童謠集繪製插畫，不少赫赫有名的插畫家都參與那項出版計畫，維特惠思卻以明快、清新的畫風脫穎而出；　他的聲名扶搖直上，很快就發展成故事、插畫一手包辦的繪本作家。

1973年《好心的怪獸》(Het goedige Monster)開啟早期系列作品，粗輪廓線條、平塗色塊的樸拙手法，塑造出鮮明的維特惠思風格；維特惠思創造的超人氣角色—小青蛙「弗洛格」，也從1980年代《好心的怪獸》(Het goedige Monster)系列中的配角，轉變成有思想、有感情的核心主角，自1989年《弗洛格戀愛了》(Kikker is verliefd)開始擔綱主演系列故事。

平凡的綠色小青蛙弗洛格，就像每個成長中的孩子，日常生活總會遇到困惑與難題，在好朋友的陪伴下，一起度過即使有挫折也無比美好的童年。

2004年國際安徒生大獎評審團，一致推崇維特惠思不僅是才華洋溢的藝術家、插畫家，且用他的創作撫慰了成長中的兒童心靈，為他們樹立足以面對往後人生的正向價值觀。

評審團主席葛瑞特(Jeffrey Garrett)指出，維特惠思的作品披著寓言的外衣，卻不像《伊索寓言》諷刺人性的愚蠢、吝嗇與虛榮，而在闡揚人性的高尚、愛與友情的力量，每一個生命個體都具有獨一無二的價值。

「真實人生並不是好萊塢的世界，弗洛格也不是超級英雄。」葛瑞特說：「維特惠思從沒拒絕承認，人生不盡如人意，難免危機、悲傷，甚至隱藏著仇恨與暴力，但只要不放棄信念，一定可以找到黑暗通往光明另一面的幽徑；　友情的鼓勵使得一切都變得可能，因為你比想像中更強大，因為你不是孤獨一人。」

這位獲獎無數的多產繪本大師，2003年舉辦80歲回顧大展，翌年獲頒國際安徒生插畫大獎桂冠，2005年1月25日病逝，83年的精采人生結束於創作生涯的巔峰。

"Frog" and his friends are the most popular characters in all characters which are created by Max Velthuijs. The brightness of its colours and the plainness of the visual style have made a warm, wisdom-included and humorous world. It expresses a peaceful love and harmony built jointly by human beings, animals and the nature.

Velthuijs was born in The Hadge on 1923. He studied painting and graphic design at Academie voor Beeldende Kunsten in Arnhem. His study had been interrupted due to World War II. After World War II, Velthuijs came back to The Hadge to paint political printings, and he also received orders of printing posters, stamps, books' covers, animations and advertisements. After those practical experiences, Velthuijs found the vocation which he wants to devote by his lifetime is painting and design for books.

In 1960s, Velthuijs concentrated on developing his talent in painting to become an illustrator. He painted for a collection of nursery rhymes published by a Dutch publisher. There were some far-famed illustrators were recruited in the plan. Velthuijs had been noticed by his bright and freshening style. His reputation has been built. He became an author both in articles and illustrations of picture books in a very short time.

Het goedige Monster is the first book of his early series. The thick outlines, flat color applications created an impressive "Velthuijs's style". The super-star "Frog", a little frog has been transformed from a supporting role in *Het goedige Monster* in 1980s to a leading character which is thinking and sentimental. It has been painted as the leading role in *Kikker is verliefd* since 1989.

Frog, a normal little frog, is just like every growing child who always faces new confusions and difficulties in his/her living. Accompanying with friends, kids would have their wonderful memories of childhoods even if there are frustrations.

The jury of the Hans Christian Andersen Awards for illustration admires Velthuijs not only for being a talented artist and illustrator. His creations also heal children's spirits and build positive values for their future life.

The jury chairman, Jeffrey Garrett, said that Velthuijs's illustrations are seen like parables. But rather than describing people's foolishness, stinginess and vanity like *Aesop's Fables*, he describes the strength of magnificence, love and friendship. Every person has the unique value.

"The real life is not like stories described in Hollywood. Frog is not a superhero, neither." "Man proposes, God disposes. Velthuijs never refuses that quote. You can't avoid risks and sadness in your life, even you will face hatred and violence. But if you keep the faith, you will find the hidden route from darkness to brightness. The encourage given by friends makes everything become possible. You will be stronger than you thought due to throwing loneliness.", said by Jeffrey Garrett.

This prolific master who has won numerous awards held the his own retrospective exhibition, 1924-2003 in 2003. He won the golden award of the Hans Christian Andersen Awards in the next year. And he passed away on Jan 25th, 2005. The final scene sets a wonderful end in his brilliant 83-year-long life.

De jongen en de vis
男孩和魚

Kikker is bang
害怕的弗洛格

Klein-Mannetje vindt het geluk
幸運的一天

Klein-Mannetje vindt het geluk
幸運的一天

Kikker en een bijzondere dag
特別的日子

Het rode kippetje
紅母雞

沃夫艾卜赫
WOLF ERLBRUCH

德國　GERMANY

2006

離開這個世界是什麼感覺？死亡很可怕嗎？德國繪本大師沃夫艾卜赫(1948-)以一種詩意而哲學的方式，用鴨子遇到死神的故事，告訴孩子：「生和死都是生命的一部分….」

艾卜赫生於德國魯爾區的烏帕塔(Wuppertal)，這處距離科隆半小時車程的中型城市，艾卡赫在此完成平面設計學業，從事雜誌插畫工作，並成為烏帕塔大學的插畫教授。

直到1985年，艾卜赫才首度嘗試童書創作，接受出版社委託，為非洲迦納政治運動領袖阿格雷(James Aggrey)創作的寓言故事《不想飛的鷹》(Der Adler, der nicht fliegen wollte)繪製插畫；當時，艾卜赫的兒子里歐納(Leonard)才剛出生，為了日後孩子可以自豪地說：「看！我老爸又畫了一本童書！」艾卜赫走上自寫自畫繪本之路。

艾卜赫的創作靈感，經常來自陪伴兒子成長的過程；他的兒子里歐納耳濡目染，長大之後也成為插畫家。

藝術底蘊深厚，艾卜赫的繪本極富藝術性，具有德國威瑪風格的色調，運用拼貼與複合媒材創作，時而簡練明快，時而錯綜複雜，令人聯想到德國超現實主義藝術家恩斯特(Max Ernst)與畢卡索、達利，乃至15世紀荷蘭畫家波希(Bosch)的怪誕幻想世界。艾卜赫融合各家之長，創造出幽默、慧黠，帶有獨特超現實氛圍的畫風，已形成追隨者眾的「艾卜赫風格」。

艾卜赫從不避諱在童書中探討嚴肅的生命議題，「孩子絕非無知，只是大人喜歡這麼想，實際上恰恰相反。」他寫著：「大人活在太多限制中，以致於無法捉摸孩子所能認知的深度。」

《我為什麼在這裡》(The Big Question)這本書中，當孩子這麼問時，哥哥說為了慶祝生日，奶奶說為了給她疼寵，媽媽說因為爸媽相愛，死亡說為了讓你更愛生命….，艾卜赫透過多元的答案，讓小朋友明白：每個人的存在，對於不同的人都有獨一無二的價值與意義。艾卜赫還在書中留下空白頁，開放這個問題。讓孩子可以隨著成長的腳步，在不同生命階段寫下不同的答案。

艾卜赫的深刻哲思，也吸引具有童心的大人，早年作品《邁爾太太放輕鬆》(Mrs Meyer the Bird)被改編成具有戲劇張力的舞台劇。而在2006年獲頒國際安徒生大獎之後，艾卜赫的創作更上層樓，2007年作品《當鴨子遇見死神》(Ente, Tod und Tulpe)柔軟、溫暖而感傷的生命教材，打動無數的世人，贏得佳評如潮。

What's the feeling of leaving the world? Is death scaring? The Germany master of picture books, Wolf Erlbruch used a philosophical and poetic way to tell children: "Both birth and death are parts of life." by the story describing an encounter between a duck and a Death.

Erlbruch was born in Wuppertal, a middle city located at Ruhr region. It's only half an hour to Cologne by driving. Erlbrush finished his study of graphic design in Wuppertal. He drew illustrations for magazines, and became a professor of illustration in University of Wuppertal .

Until 1985, Erlbruch started drawing children's books. He was under contract with publishers for painting illustrations in a parable: *"Der Adler, der nicht fliegen wollte"* to memorize James Aggrey, a political leader in Ghana, Africa. At the time, his son Leonard was just born. In order to make his son to feel great sense of pride for him and say: "Look! My father has finished another childern's book!" in the future, he stepped on the road of creating his own picture books.

The creations of Erlbruch are inspired by the experiences of taking care of his son. His son Leonard has been imbued by his father and become an illustrator as well.

His great artistic virtue makes Erlbruch's picture books be deeply artistic which express the color style of Weimar culture. He creates creations by composite media and collage techniques which make his style sometimes bright and vivid, sometimes complicated and mixed. It makes people think about Max Ernst, the Germany artist of surrealism, Picasso and Dali. And it also could be associated to the freaky imagination of the Dutch painter, Bosch in 15th century. Erlbruch has combined different advantages from different fields to create a humorous, clever and surrealistic style. He has established a "Erlbrush's style" and recruited lots followers.

Erlbruch never escapes from discussing life issues in his books. "Kids are not ignorant. Adults always deem that, but the fact is opposite." "There are too many chains to make adults figure out the deepness of children's mind."

In *The Big Question*, the kid asked the question. His brother said the answer is for celebrating his birthday. His grandmother said the answer is for giving him love. His mother said the reason is the deep love between his parents. The Death said it makes people cherish their lives. The diversified answers are describes by Erlbruch to make children know: "Each person has his/her own unique meaning and value toward different persons." Erlbruch leave a blank page in the book to open the answer of the question. Every child could write down his/her answer in the different stage of his/her life with the growth.

The philosophic thinking of Erlbruch attracts adults who embrace their childlike innocence. His early creation *Mrs Meyer the Bird* has been rewrote to a theatrical stage drama. After the qualification by the Hans Christian Andersen Awards for illustration in 2006, he makes a great progress in his creations. The soft, warm and moving story as a life education of *Ente, Tod und Tulpe* has struck numerous people and received rave reviews from the world.

Duck, Death and the Tulip
當鴨子遇上死神

131/200

Schon wieder was !
又是什麼！
沃夫艾卜赫 Wolf Erlbruch

英諾桑提
ROBERTO INNOCENTI

義大利　ITALY

2008

戰爭結束了，小女孩的媽媽卻一直等不到女兒回家，集中營的鐵絲網上，一朵枯萎的小花，柔弱，卻撼動人心！

義大利插畫家英諾桑提(1940-)未曾受過學院繪畫訓練，自學成家的他，卻透過細膩寫實的畫面，帶引讀者親臨他所經歷過的大時代巨變。

英諾桑提在二次世界大戰期間，生於義大利托斯卡尼的小城巴尼奧阿里波利(Bagno a Ripoli)，13歲輟學成為鋼鐵廠工人以貼補家用。後來，他到羅馬一家動畫工作室工作，在實務經驗中磨練出一手精湛的插畫技藝，並搬回佛羅倫斯，從事電影、戲劇的海報、書籍封面設計工作。

1970年，受到美國知名插畫家約翰‧奧爾康(John Alcorn)鼓勵，英諾桑提開始嘗試童書繪本創作。1983年接受委任繪製《灰姑娘》，英諾桑提將人物與故事背景改為1920年代的英國村莊，以現代精神重新詮釋經典，從此聲名鵲起，創作《小木偶奇遇記》、《小氣財神》、《胡桃鉗》等經典名作插畫。

英諾桑提擅長以精細描繪的功力，呈現全景式的逼真場景，充滿敘事性的藝術風格，寫實中帶有濃厚的象徵主義詩情，非常引人入勝，而他最膾炙人口的代表作，首推1985年作品《鐵絲網上的小花》(Rose Blanche)。

《鐵絲網上的小花》由瑞士記者暨作家葛拉茲(Christophe Gallaz)撰文、英諾桑提繪圖，描寫二次大戰的德國小鎮、名叫露絲‧白蘭奇(Rose Blanche)的小女孩，無意中發現好幾個瘦弱小孩，穿著有一顆紅星的條紋衣，被關在一處鐵絲網後的木屋裡；白蘭奇常常省下麵包去探望他們，為此越來越瘦。有一天，白蘭奇到了老地方卻看不到那些孩子，她摘了一朵花放在鐵絲網上，而後，一陣槍聲響起，白蘭奇從此沒有回家；第二年春天，野地的花兒遍開，鐵絲網上的小花卻早已枯萎…。

露絲‧白蘭奇是「Rose Blanche」的音譯，原意「白玫瑰」，實則影射二次大戰期間，一群以「白玫瑰」為名進行反納粹地下運動，卻被蓋世太保殺害的德國年輕人。《鐵絲網上的小花》沒有激烈控訴，沒有寫出「一顆紅星的條紋衣」是猶太人在集中營的囚服，也沒有直指白蘭奇的犧牲，但無論大人小孩，看到最後一頁都會忍不住流淚。

「在這本書裡，我想要表達的，就是一個親眼看過戰爭的孩子，如何體驗戰爭中的種種無奈、悲哀和矛盾，又如何能在戰火中，體會永不磨滅的人性光輝。」英諾桑提以這個故事揭露法西斯主義的真面目，卻沒有透過仇恨的手段，而是在哀傷中注入省思，以愛來形塑希望。

The war is over. But the mother still doesn't see her girl. A withered flower, winded on the barbed wire, is weak, but heart-moving!

The Italian illustrator, Roberto Innocenti is never educated by academic painting training. He learned the skills by self-study. The realistic and delicate scenes bring readers to experience the incredible changes of the times.

Innocenti was born in a small town, Bagno a Ripoli located in Tuscany during World War II. He dropped his study and became a worker in a steelworks to help his family at 13. He transferred and worked in an animation studio afterwards. His practical experiences make his masterly painting skills. Then he moved to Florence and did some film posters and books' cover design.

Innocenti was encouraged by a American famous illustrator, John Alcom, to start painting children's books. He was employed for painting *Cinderella*. Innocenti changed the background into an England village in 1920s. He interpreted the classic by a modern spirit and gained a great renown. He painted the illustrations for the classics like *The Adventures of Pinocchio*, *A Christmas Carol* and *The Nutcracke*r.

Innocenti is talented in detailed painting to represent panoramic realistic scenes. The artistic style with narrative describing, the realistic style with Symbolism poetry are very attracting people. The most popular masterpiece of course is *Rose Blanche* created in 1985.

The articles of *Rose Blanche* were written by a Switzerland reporter and author Christophe Gallaz, and the pictures were painted by Innocenti. The story describes a girl named Rose Blanche who lived in a Germany village during World War II. She accidently noticed some skinny kids wearing striped clothing with a red star who were locked in a woodhouse behind barbed wire. Blanche saved her bread for them, and she had been getting thinner and thinner. One day Blanche went to the house but she didn't see any kid there. She plucked a little flower and stuck it on the wire. After that, the sound of gunshots was heard. Blanche never came home since that day. In the next spring, flowers on the field were blooming, but the flower on the wire was withering...

The meaning of Rose Blanche is "white rose". It represents the anti-Nazi group "White Rose" formed by young people who were killed by Gestapo during World War II. There is no fierce accusation in *Rose Blanche*. There is no description saying that the clothing with a red star is the prison clothing of Jews. There is no direct sentence describing the sacrifice of Blanche. But no matter an adult or a kid, everyone will cry when they see the last page.

"In this book, I want to express how a war-experienced child undergoes unwillingness, sadness and contradictions, and how the child realizes the glory of human nature." Innocenti brings Fascism to light by the story. Rather than some hatred ways, he chooses adding awareness into sadness and using love to build hope.

尤塔鮑爾
JUTTA BAUER

德國　GERMANY

2010

「嚇得魂飛魄散」或許是形容詞，德國繪本天后尤塔鮑爾 (1955-) 卻畫出小企鵝因為企鵝媽媽的大吼大叫，嚇得身體都四分五裂了，提醒家長小心情緒暴力帶來的傷害。

尤塔鮑爾從出生以來，一直定居在德國第二大城漢堡，父親是農校老師，家中有10個兄弟姐妹，快樂大家庭出身的她，非常重視家族的愛與緊密關係，帶來的正向力量，她所創作的故事題材，也大多來自濃濃的親情。

2010年鮑爾獲頒國際安徒生大獎時，就曾指出，她的書中藏有許多她所愛的人，2009年獲德國青少年文學插畫特別獎的繪本《爺爺的天使》(El Angel del Albuelo)，述說的是她爺爺和奶奶 (天使) 的故事，鮑爾書中的企鵝、熊、小孩，則大多與她摯愛的獨子賈斯柏 (Jasper) 有關。

鮑爾1981年畢業於漢堡應用藝術學院後，即從事童書繪本工作。早年她與多位作家合作，尤其為德國作家波伊 (Kirsten Boie) 繪製《七月男孩尤里》(Juli) 系列最受矚目，不過，鮑爾越來越覺得「自己創作文字和圖畫比較好玩，那是一個屬於自己的世界。」

2001年獲得德國青少年文學獎的作品《大吼大叫的企鵝媽媽》(Schreimutter)，就是鮑爾第一本自寫自畫的繪本。由於白天生氣罵了兒子，鮑爾在那晚的床邊故事，編了企鵝媽媽向小企鵝說對不起，來與兒子和解。「要教導孩子是非對錯，我們不是完美的父母，也會犯錯，重要的是，向孩子道歉，才是身教。」

有趣的是，或許「小企鵝的身體四分五裂」太驚悚，起初沒有出版社感興趣，沒想到書一出就大轟動，媒體盛讚鮑爾用極簡的圖文與留白，生動傳達了親子日常互動強大的情緒張力，甚至有兒童心理研究指出，面對強大暴力的孩子，確實會想像自己的身體四分五裂、好像被毀掉了一樣。

鮑爾創作時，並不會特別設想是要畫給小孩看的童書。《幸福是什麼》(Selma) 其實是給大人看的故事，《顏色女王大考驗》(Die Koenigen der Farben) 也不是專為小孩而畫，「好故事本身沒有設限。」她說。

近年鮑爾與德國歌德學院合作，常到世界各地舉辦孩子的故事工作坊，影響她的創作重要性與日俱增。鮑爾更清楚認知到：說故事是每個人與生俱來的能力，孩子在故事中發出疑問、解決問題、建構世界，在故事的發展中可以看到孩子的原創力和想像力，大人卻慢慢遺失了這個美好的能力。

"Somebody was frightened out of his wits." Maybe it is just a metaphor. But Jutta Bauer, the queen of picture books in Germany, drew a little penguin's body falling apart due to the yelling from its mother. It notices parents to aware the hurt by emotion violence.

She resides in the 2nd biggest city in Germany, Hamburg since she was born. Her father is a teacher in an agricultural school. She has 10 siblings. Growing up in a happy big family makes her very respect on the positive power brought by love and close relationship in family. The materials of her creations usually originate from great family love.

At the moment she received the Hans Christian Andersen Awards for illustration in 2010. She stated that she hid many people whom are loved by her in books. She won the Special prize of German Youth Literature Prize for *El Angel del Albuelo* which describes the story between her grandfather and grandmother (the angel). Most of the penguins, bears and kids in Bauer's creations are related to her only son, Jasper whom is deeply loved by her.

After her graduation from the Technical College of Design in Hamburg, she paints for children's picture books. In the early stage, she worked with some authors. The most popular creation is the series for *Juli* with a Germany author, Kirsten Boie. But after this stage, Bauer thinks "It'll be my own world and more interesting, if I create all of articles and illustrations by myself only." more and more confidently.

She won the German Youth Literature Prize in 2001 for the picture book *Schreimutter* which articles and illustrations are created by herself. Because she blamed on her child in day, she created the bedtime story which talks about a mommy penguin saying sorry to her little for seeking a compromise with her son. "We should teach children something right or wrong. We're not perfect. We'll make mistakes. The important thing is saying sorry to your kid when that happened. That makes you become a right model."

The interesting thing is that perhaps a little penguin's body falling apart is too scaring to attract publishers' attention at first. Nobody could predict the great sensation right after its publishing. Journalisms admire Bauer's vivid expressions of the powerful tension in the interactions between parents and children by her clean illustrations, sentences and blank sites. Some researches of children's psychology support that children will image their bodies being tearing or ruining when they're facing strong violence.

She never sets up her creations for adults or kids previously when she is painting. *Selma* is a story for adults actually. *Die Koenigen der Farben* is not for kids, neither. "A good story never sets a limitation." She said.

Recently Bauer collaborates with the Goethe-Institut for holding story workshops in the world which progressively affects her creations. Bauer more clearly realizes that saying a story in an innate talent for everybody. Children find questions. Then they solve questions and contribute their world. We can see the creativity and imagination of kids from the textures of stories. But adults are losing those amazing talents.

Selma
幸福是什麼？

Opas Engel
爺爺的天使

Opas Engel
爺爺的天使

Schreimutter
大吼大叫的企鵝媽媽

彼德席斯
PETER SÍS

捷克　CZECH-REPUBLIC

2012

「如果你順利的找到鑰匙，解開布拉格之謎，那我就可以説一些歷史，講一些故事給你聽，但你必須自己決定，是不是真的想知道。也許你會找到幾顆我遺失的彈珠，也許會聽到我童年時代所聽慣的熟悉鐘聲。如果你有時間耐心品味，你將會發現，布拉格是個魔法城。」

一個流亡異國的藝術家，一段永遠回不去的鄉愁，美籍捷克插畫大師彼德席斯（1949- ）為他的女兒瑪德蓮寫下《三隻金鑰匙》（The Three Golden Keys），記述布拉格傳説，即使當時女兒還太小，根本無法體會父親的心情。

彼德席斯1949年生於蘇聯占領下的捷克斯洛伐克，成長於共產黨統治下的鐵幕，席斯説：「人們無法選擇在和平或戰亂中生存，但能夠在一個痛苦的年代裡，像孩子般玩耍是很幸運且美好的事，回想起來，我有個很棒的童年都要歸功於我親愛的父母。」席斯的父親是電影製片人，母親是藝術家，他們都鼓勵席斯去追尋自己的藝術和夢想。父親因特殊身份得以在鐵幕外旅行，席斯由他所帶回的遠方故事開啟想像，並得以在布拉格應用藝術學院畢業後，前往倫敦皇家藝術學院深造，受教於著名插畫家昆丁布雷克（Quentin Blake）。完成學業之後，席斯投入電影工作，1980年就以動畫短片《頭》（Hlavy）贏得柏林影展「金熊獎」，並於1982年赴美，籌備1984年洛杉磯奧運影片，後因東歐國家集體抵制奧運，捷克政府電召席斯回國，當時他正為鮑伯狄倫製作MV，毅然決定留在美國，尋求政治庇護。滯美之後，席斯因拍攝影片不符美國觀眾口味，轉而創作童書繪本，迄今已八度獲紐約時報年度繪本獎，不僅是2012年國際安徒生大獎得主，百餘年歷史的美國插畫家學會（Society of Illustrators）也於2015年頒予他終生成就獎。

席斯創作的繪本相當豐富，有為孩子寫的《小女兒長大了》、《我有一隻狗》以及一首首恐龍詩、玩想像遊戲的類型。最典型的席斯繪本，則是《跟著夢想前進：哥倫布》、《生命之樹－達爾文的一生》、《伽利略：星星的使者》等傳記類作品，以及用他的父親早年寄自西藏的書信創作出的《天諭之地》、為下一代記錄故鄉布拉格傳奇的《三隻金鑰匙》。

這些傳記類繪本，或具有自傳色彩的作品，圖像都極其細膩繁複，細節考證講究，帶有中世紀的神秘氛圍，令人不由得沈迷於隱藏其中的密碼和玄機。國際安徒生大獎評審團盛讚彼德·席斯是擅長多種複合媒材的大師，運用強大想像力，創造出錯綜複雜的視覺語彙，形成彼德·席斯獨樹一幟的非凡魅力。

"If you find the keys for the secret of Prague, I can tell you some history, some stories. Do you really want to know or not? It's up to you. Perhaps you'll find some marbles I leave. Perhaps you'll hear the familiar bell tones in my childhood. You'll find that Prague is a magic city, if you have time to taste it."

An exiling artist, a nostalgia in the history, the American Czech illustration master Peter Sís wrote *The Three Golden Keys* for his daughter Madeleine to describe the legends in Prague, even if his daughter was too young to understand her father's feeling.

Peter Sís was born in Czechoslovakia which was occupied by the Soviet Union in 1949. He grew up in the Iron Curtain. The area was ruled by Communists. Sís said: "People couldn't choose to be born in peace or in a war. But I could play like a normal child in the misery. It's lucky and wonderful. When I think of it, my great childhood should refer to my dear parents."

Sís's father was a filmmaker. His mother was an artist. Both of them encouraged Sís to chase his own dream and artistic way. His father could travel outside of the Iron Curtain due to his special identity. Sís started his imagination from the overseas stories brought by his father. And he could continue his study in the Royal College of Art in London after his graduation from the Academy of Applied Arts in Prague. He was taught by a famous illustrator, Quentin Blake.

After he finished his study, he devoted himself to film production. He won a Golden Bear Award for an animated short, *Hlavy*, at the 1980 Berlin International Film Festival. He came to America in 1982 for producing the movie for 1984 Summer Olympics in Los Angeles. Due to the boycott by eastern Europe countries, the Czech government called Sís for coming back. In the meanwhile, he was producing a music video for Bob Dylan and decided to stay in American firmly and sought for political asylum.

Because his films don't match the taste of Americans, he changed to create children's picture books after his staying. Until now, he has received the New York Times Book Review Best Illustrated Book of the Year award for eight times. He is not only the winner of the Hans Christian Andersen Awards for illustration in 2012. He also received the Original Art Lifetime Achievement Award 2015 from the Society of Illustrators which has built its reputation over 100 years.

There are various styles of his books. There is a style which is created for kids like *Madlenka*, *Madlenka's Dog*. It also includes the books describing dinosaur poems or imaginary games. The classic style of Sís's books is a biography books like *Follow the Dream : The Story of Christopher Columbus, The Tree of Life: Charles Darwin and Starry Messenger*. Other classics of Sis are Tibet which is inspired by his father's mails to *Tibet* and *The Three Golden Keys*, the record of the legends in his hometown Prague for offspring.

The common characters of those biography or autobiography books are the detailed pictures, complete history studies and a mysterious atmosphere like in the middle ages. Those make people enjoy in searching the hidden codes or secrets. The jury of the Hans Christian Andersen Awards for illustration admires Peter Sís as a master in composite media. He uses his powerful imagination to create complicated visual language which forms his exclusively own and incredible fascination.

Untitled (Whale)
無題 (鯨魚)

Untitled (Skunk)
無題 (臭鼬)

Untitled (Penguin)
無題 (企鵝)

Untitled (Amerka,Amerka 1), 1991
無題(美國，美國1)

Untitled (Amerka,Amerka 2), 1991
無題 (美國，美國2)

羅傑梅洛
ROGER MELLO

巴西　BRAZIL

2014

2014年國際安徒生大獎頒予巴西插畫家羅傑梅洛 (1965-　)，是史上第一位獲得這項殊榮的拉丁美洲創作者。

羅傑梅洛擊敗31名對手脫穎而出，評審團主席吉爾 (María Jesús Gil) 指出，2014年的文學獎得主上橋菜穗子 (日本)、插畫家得主羅傑梅洛 (巴西)，都是來自遠方的國度，也同樣帶來重要的訊息：透過他們的作品，告訴所有的大人與小孩，我們應該追求更美好的世界。

1965年生於巴西首都巴西利亞，梅洛自稱是「在軍事鎮壓與思想控制的年代長大的孩子」。巴西自1964至1985年是「軍事獨裁時期」，長達二十餘年的高壓統治，梅洛的童年沒有迪士尼、沒有超級英雄，只能在封閉社會中自行發揮天馬行空的想像力。

「當年巴西有許多才華洋溢、思想自由奔放的建築師、設計師及畫家，但他們隨時都可能因為擁有禁書而遭受迫害，或惹來殺身之禍。」梅洛說：「這樣的社會氛圍，也讓我認知到書籍與思想的力量。而這些前輩的圖像創作，對我個人藝術養成多有啟發。」

梅洛認為，多虧了上一代思想家與藝術家，使巴西在嚴峻時代仍保有一小片桃源淨土，而他就是「烏托邦與絕望拉鋸下的那一代產物」。

擁有工業設計學位，梅洛著有上百件作品，涵蓋詩集、短篇小說、劇本以及童書繪本。他的故事經常取材自巴西民間故事與傳說，融合拉丁美洲嘉年華式的繽紛色彩，以及抽象表現主義、立體派、歐普藝術等現代藝術風格，創造出極其強烈的視覺語彙。

成長於威權時代，梅洛總是透過畫作傳達濃厚的社會批判，試圖喚起省思。《小燒炭工》(Carvoeirinhos) 就是控訴無情資本家剝削童工累積財富的悲慘世界，《紅樹林的孩子》(Meninos do mangue) 則是描述住在紅樹林的孩子，必須趁著潮汐捕捉魚蟹以維生，梅洛說：「這本書設定在不常見的場景，卻是許多孩子賴以生存的家，而他們都是被社會忽視的小孩。」

看不慣不公不義，梅洛甚至創作《祖貝爾與迷宮》(Zubair e os Labrintos) 以控訴2003年美軍入侵伊拉克，掠奪巴格達的國家博物館數千件文物。耐人尋味的是，梅洛在國際間聲名日隆，唯獨美國未曾出版他的書，也沒有任何英文版問世。

梅洛的人道主義精神，則在歐洲備受推崇，巴黎圖書館還將他的《紅樹林的孩子》等數本作品，選為「踏入成人世界前必讀之書」。

The Hans Christian Andersen Awards for illustration 2014 went to Roger Mello who is the first winner from Latin America in the history.

Roger Mello has been selected in 32 nominees. The jury chairman, María Jesús Gil said the winner of writing award from Japan (Nahoko Uehashi) and the winner of illustration award from Brazil (Roger Mello),are both from very far countries. That sent an important message: via their creations, we should chase for a better world, no matter adults or children.

Mello was born in Brasilia, the capital of Brazil in 1965. He said he was a boy who grew up in the era of mind control and military suppression. Brazil was under the military regime from 1964 to 1985. The coercion lasted more than 20 years. There was no Disney, no superhero in Mello's childhood. Only thing he could do is his own imagination in the closed society.

"There were many talented and free-minding architects, designers and painters in Brazil. But they might be killed or abused due to having a banned book." "This social atmosphere let me realize the power of books and thoughts. The graphic creations by predecessors have inspired me in many faces." Mello said.

Mello thinks that the pure land is protected by last generation's thinkers and artists in the coercionary era. He is the new birth of the generation "under a struggle between Utopian and despair".

Mello has a degree of industrial design. He has created more than 100 creations including poetry, short novels, scripts and children's picture books. His ideas are usually from Brazilian folklores or legends. The colorful colors from carnival styles in Latin America and some modern arts like abstract expressionism, cubism and optical art are merged into his creations to create a very intense visual language.

Because he grew up in the age of authoritarianism, Mello always criticizes the society by his painting to arouse some awareness. *Carvoeirinhos* accuses the cruel capitalists who exploit child labors for gathering wealth. *Meninos do mangue* describes children who live in red forests and feed themselves by capturing fishes and crabs. "The scenario is set at an unusual site. But that is a real residence for many kids who are ignored by the society." Mello said.

He is always indignant on injustice. Mello created *Zubair e os Labrintos* for accusing the plundering of thousands relics from the National Museum of Iraq in 2003 invasion of Iraq. The most intriguing thing is that there is no any publishing of his creations in America. And there is no English version in the world neither even though he has become more and more famous.

Mello's spirit of humanitarianism has gained high reputation in Europe. Libraries in Paris have selected his creations including *Meninos do mangue* as "the must-read books before you became an adult".

Nau Catarineta 1
卡塔利那船

Tomou-o um anjo nos braços,
não o deixou afogar.
Deu um estouro o demônio,
acalmaram vento e mar.
E à noite, a nau Catarineta
a bom porto foi parar.

Calou-se o Capitão,
que terra clara se via;
e a marujada, contente,
qual a qual assim dizia:

AS CASINHAS QUE LÁ HÁ
BEM AS VEMOS A ALVEJAR.
DAS LAREIRAS QUE ELAS TÊM
NÓS BEM VEMOS FUMEGAR.
AS PADEIRAS QUE LÁ MORAM
BEM AS VEMOS PADEJAR.
FRITADEIRAS QUE LÁ VIVEM
PEIXINHOS ESTÃO A FRITAR.
AS TABERNEIRAS SENTIMOS
DA PIPA VINHO A TIRAR.
ANDA, NAU CATARINETA,
QUE LÁ JÁ VAMOS JANTAR!

Nau Catarineta 3
卡塔利那船

Meninos do Mangue 1
男孩曼格

Todo Cuidado é Pouco!
所有微小的關心！

國際安徒生插畫大獎50周年展
Hans Christian Andersen Awards 50th Anniversary Exibition

2016/06/25-2016/09/18
國立中正紀念堂　National Chiang Kai-shek Memorial Hall

國家圖書館出版品預行編目(CIP)資料

國際安徒生插畫大獎50周年展/ 胡忻儀總編輯. -- 臺北市：蔚龍藝術, 民105.06
　面；　公分
　ISBN　978-986-88025-8-2（平裝）

1.插畫 2.作品集

947.45　　　　　　　　　　　　105010641

發行人　　　　王玉齡
展覽顧問　　　Michael Neugebauer
總編輯　　　　胡忻儀
企畫編輯　　　張又予、畢明媛
美術編輯　　　呂碧蓉
內文　　　　　蔚龍藝術有限公司、IBBY
出版單位　　　蔚龍藝術有限公司
　　　　　　　臺北市大同區迪化街一段127號
　　　　　　　02-2550-6775
　　　　　　　www.bluedragonart.com.tw
出版日期　　　中華民國105年6月24日
定價　　　　　新台幣1000元
ISBN　　　　　978-986-88025-8-2

Publisher　　　　　　　Yuling Wang
Exhibition Consultant　Michael Neugebauer
Editoral Team　　　　 Hsinyi Hu, Yu-yu Chang, Yuan Pi
Design　　　　　　　　Bi-Rong Lu
Content Text　　　　　Blue Dragon Art Company, IBBY

Blue Dragon Art Company
No.127, Sec. 1, Dihua St, Datong Dist, Taipei City 103, Taiwan, R.O.C
+886-2-2550-6775
www.bluedragonart.com.tw
Date of Publication: 24 June, 2016

主辦單位 Organizer：　國立中正紀念堂管理處 NATIONAL CHIANG KAI-SHEK MEMORIAL HALL 、 三立媒體集團 、 閣林文創股份有限公司 GREENLAND CREATIVE CO., LTD. 、 iBbY

策劃單位 Planner：　蔚龍藝術有限公司 Blue Dragon Art Company

版權所有，未經許可不得刊印或轉載（缺頁或破損書籍，請寄回更換）

特別感謝 Special thanks to all participants：
IBBY, Alois Carigiet, Klemens Kluge, Jiří Trnka, Maurice Sendak, Eric Carle Museum of Picture Book Art, Ib Spang Olsen, Rolf Vedel Petersen, Farshid Mesghali, Kanoon International Affairs, Tatjana Mawrina, Svend Otto, Suekichi Akaba, Chihiro Art Museum Azumino, Zbigniew Rychlicki, Andrzej Rychlicki, Mitsumasa Anno, Anno Art Museum, Robert Ingpen, minedition, 格林文化事業股份有限公司GRIMM PRESS LTD., Dušan Kállay, Lisbeth Zwerger, Květa Pacovská, Jörg Müller, Klaus Ensikat, Tomi Ungerer, Anthony Browne, Walker Books, Quentin Blake, Max Velthuijs, Letterkundig Museum, Wolf Erlbruch, Jutta Bauer, Peter Sís, Mary Ryan Gallery, Roger Mello

圖像版權 Image Copyright：
©IBBY, Alois Carigiet, Jiří Trnka, Maurice Sendak, Ib Spang Olsen, Svend Otto, Mitsumasa Anno, Tomi Ungerer ©Galleri Ib Spang Olsen, Ib Spang Olsen ©Kanoon International Affairs, Farshid Mesghali ©minedition, Tatjana Mawrina, Jörg Müller, Květa Pacovská ©Chihiro Art Museum Azumino, Suekichi Akaba ©Zbigniew Rychlicki, Zbigniew Rychlicki ©Robert Ingpen ©Dušan Kállay ©Lisbeth Zwerger ©Květa Pacovská ©Klaus Ensikat ©Anthony Browne ©Chris Beetles Gallery, Quentin Blake ©Letterkundig Museum, Max Velthuijs ©Klemens Kluge, Wolf Erlbruch ©Jutta Bauer ©Mary Ryan Gallery, Peter Sís ©Roger Mello